THE SIMPLE LIFE IS MURDER

ANNE BARTON

The Simple Life is Murder
Anne Barton

Copyright Anne Barton 2017

Carrick Publishing
Print Edition 2017
ISBN 13: 978-1-77242-078-4
Cover Design by Sara Carrick
Author Photo by Maia MacDonald
Print Edition, License Notes:

This book is intended for your personal enjoyment only. This book may not be sold or given away to other people. If you did not purchase this book, or it was not purchased for your use only, then please purchase your own copy. Thank you for respecting the hard work of this author.

The people, places and events in this story are entirely fictional.

Chapter One

I was thirteen, about to turn fourteen, and my sister was eleven, when our parents moved to Beaver Creek. Phillip and Elizabeth Taylor were kidded that they should have named their children Charles and Anne. They didn't. They named us Derek and Penny. We were impressionable enough to agree with enthusiasm when our parents decided to move out into the wilderness to lead 'the simple life.' Well, let me tell you, life in the wilderness isn't so simple.

It's tough adjusting to life where you have to do *everything* yourself when you are used to just picking up the phone and calling someone to do it. In the first place, no phone! Also, as Penny and I discovered when we were confined to the tent we were temporarily living in by three days of steady pouring rain, no TV and no computers!

We had been brainwashed into thinking that we were going to have life experiences that would stand us in good stead in the future. I'll admit that we did learn some things that most kids never have a chance to do—how to milk a cow, split wood, dig post holes, sharpen a crosscut saw, and how a mother animal, including a human one, calls her young in times of danger. I'm not quite sure how these things are supposed to help us in everyday life.

There were more exciting things also. A neighbour boy showed me how to catch fish illegally right under the nose of the conservation officer. Along with him, I also learned how to use chewing tobacco and where the marijuana was grown.

Mom was Canadian; Dad was a US citizen. They met and married in Calgary where I was born, but Dad didn't like the oil culture of Alberta so they moved to northern Idaho by the time Penny came along. We are both dual citizens I guess. Dad was very interested in conservation and thought that living close to nature, without modern conveniences, would show everyone that it wasn't necessary to tear up the environment in order to have a happy and productive life. He also thought that getting away from city life would shield us kids from the crime that he felt was rampant on the city streets. I don't know how he convinced Mom. I think she considered it more of an adventure than a protest against modern life. For Penny and me, the prospect of not having to go trudging off to boring old school every day was exciting. We knew we could do the schoolwork in far less time than in a regular school, and Mom thought we would probably learn more.

Our early schooling was in Idaho, but when our parents went looking for a wilderness location to settle down, they checked out British Columbia as well as places in Idaho and Montana. I think the thing that decided them on BC was schooling. Mom heard that British Columbia had a system where kids could be home schooled, no matter where they lived, by registering with a school board somewhere in BC which would then provide curriculum, advice, testing, and grading. So BC it was.

We found a place just over the border and went to Caribou, a larger city, to register with the school board and get the necessary materials. School was out at the end of May at our old school in Idaho, but not until late June in BC. So Penny and I visited the schools in Caribou when we visited that city in June, to get the feel of the Canadian curriculum and meet the teachers who would guide our work. I learned that the city had been named Caribou not because those animals were common there (they live in the more Arctic regions) but because the city fathers, when the town became incorporated, wanted a better sounding name than the old one of Fitch's Folly. Fitch was an early settler, but no one knew exactly what his folly had been.

The English teacher who would guide my lessons was enthusiastic about what she called 'the simple life' and suggested that I should keep a journal and write essays based on it. I could e-mail them to her. No I couldn't, Mom told her. "Why not?" the teacher asked. "Because we won't have computers," Mom explained. (I missed that conversation or I would have been alarmed long before I got dragged out into the bush, as they call it up here.) "Can't you get a computer?" To which Mom replied that there would be no electricity. The teacher seemed completely nonplused by that.

One of the teachers who would be guiding our schoolwork said she would put us in touch with a group of home-schoolers so that we could go on field trips with other kids. Mom patiently explained that we would be too far out to be able to do so. Besides, our whole life would be one large 'field trip.'

Anyway, the idea of keeping a journal registered with me, and I did send in accounts of our life in the bush, mailing a bunch of stuff every time Dad went into town to get mail and groceries. He would pick up the teachers' replies, and Penny and I would spend hours poring over our graded lessons. We became gradually more accurate and neat, and our teachers began to praise our work, saying that it was a pleasure to work with children who really did their own work, rather than relying on Google. At one point this went to my head, but I was brought down to earth by the scathing criticism of my next lesson. I actually asked for, and got, a dictionary for Christmas. That's how badly the wilderness experience has addled my youthful brain.

Penny decided to improve her memory. She started out with poetry, and when I got tired of listening to her, she went around the place reciting verse to the cow, the cat and the horses. Later on, she practiced long multiplication and division, and had reached the point where she could multiply or divide one four-figure number by another in her head with extreme accuracy. She can add up a column of numbers in a flash, and doesn't need a calculator for anything. She started this when her hand calculator's battery went dead and I wouldn't loan her mine.

I thought maybe she might become an accountant, but she said she planned to be a veterinarian. She loves animals, so I guess this might be a good choice. I'm the one who ought to be doing all this math stuff. I want to be an engineer.

In the stories of life in the wild that I sent in to the school, I tried to explain that life in the bush wasn't so simple. What I wrote was not a how-to, but a why-not-to account of living in the wilderness. We'd been told of fields of wildflowers where you watched endless beautiful sunsets. In reality, we discovered that the beautiful sunsets were few and far between, and often concealed by rain clouds or snow, and the fields had other things in them besides wildflowers; things like gopher holes, thistles, porcupine quills and cow pies. So you didn't watch the sunsets even when they were there. You watched where you were putting your feet. The teacher said she enjoyed the humour, but I was dead serious. I edited the things I wrote for her, with the really spicy stuff left out because I didn't know how the teacher would react to accounts of some of the stuff I did.

Chapter Two

I first saw the land on Beaver Creek that was to become our home on a fine summer morning in early June. The road out there was still wet from earlier rains and we splashed through several good-sized mud puddles. By the time we got to our destination, our new silver extended-cab pickup truck was covered with mud. Mom looked at it with dismay, but Dad was delighted, saying that it now looked like a remote rancher's vehicle. Mom muttered something that sounded like, "boys and their toys."

The pickup was our one concession to modernity. Dad said he had no intention of packing everything in on horseback. He had never ridden a horse, and still has never done so, but one of the lures held out to Penny and me was that we would have a place to keep horses.

We were to set up our living quarters in a small grove of pine trees on a slight slope above the sluggish creek. Penny and I were sent out to gather up wood for our fire. We scrounged around the hillside for downed branches, dragging or carrying them back to the site where Dad, with help from a neighbour, was building a floor and framework upon which the sixteen by twenty foot tent would be erected. We spent a cold and miserable winter in that tent before our house was built.

We worked busily at making our space liveable. Bill Herman, a neighbour my parents had talked to before buying the land, saw us arrive and came over to offer his help. We hadn't lived there long before we realized that this man would invariably materialize whenever anything needed to be done. He was retired from the ranching he had done most of his adult life, running a herd of Herford cattle on the meadowland along the creek. He needed something to occupy himself, and something to do with his hands. Mom sorted out the things involved with food, giving us a picnic lunch, then making preparations for cooking and food storage. Bill Herman, the helpful neighbour, advised Mom not to store in the tent anything that might attract bears. I could see that the prospect of bears sharing our living space had not been something she had planned for, or even thought of. She reacted with a gasp of shock. Dad hadn't thought about it either. He and Bill considered the options and decided to build a small outbuilding with a door that could be secured against bears. So our larder started out in a house, while we humans lived in a tent.

We would need an outdoor toilet. Mom wanted it up behind a clump of brush so it wouldn't be visible from the tent, but Bill pointed out that it should be downhill from the house, and far enough away that we would not constantly smell it in the heat of the summer. I had numerous occasions to regret this distance when I had to make trips to it in the dead of winter. I had to help dig the pit, my first experience with hard manual labour.

In the meantime, Penny continued hauling in branches to use as firewood. She was quite proud of the big pile she had created. But then Bill commented that we only had enough wood for one day and we really did need to drag in a dead tree to saw into stove-wood lengths and split up. He knew a horse logger who lived nearby who would probably come to drag in a tree for us. The forested land above the road was part of our property and could be used as a source of wood to keep the home fire burning.

By late afternoon we were all tired from the unaccustomed work. Mom sighed, pushing a lock of sweat-dampened hair back from her forehead. "I guess I'd better think about supper. It will have to come from cans."

"Now don't you bother," Bill Herman exclaimed. "Grace expects you over for supper."

"Oh, but we can't impose on your wife like that!"

"Think nothing of it. We've been looking forward to you coming and we want to get acquainted. We don't have much company out here. We don't have much in common with the Monkes, and Stone keeps to himself." These were the other people who lived out there on Beaver Creek.

Grace Herman greeted us with hugs and exclamations of delight. She fed us a meal of roast beef with spuds and vegetables from her own garden, followed by cherry pie, the cherries having been picked from a tree in their back yard. She kept urging us to take seconds and thirds. I ate like a pig, hungry after all the heavy work I'd done. Grace seemed delighted. "Derek, you're thin. You need to eat more. Have another piece of pie."

I glanced at my mother, who had more or less rationed our food, especially sweets and junk food, fearing that we would become fat. She restrained herself from saying anything, with some difficulty I think, so I took the offered pie. When I finished eating it I couldn't have swallowed another bite. When we got back to our 'home,' Mom had some things to say about my manners. But this was by no means our last experience with the farm wife mentality—you fed your visitors with everything you could put on the table.

We eventually purchased a cow, which we were to pick up as soon as we had a pasture fenced and a place built to store hay and grain and provide shelter in bad weather. It didn't need to be fancy, we were told. The cow would do fine with just a place to get out of the rain. But the hay would have to be protected from rain and blowing snow. So again, we built an enclosed structure for the feed and merely a roof over the animal. The parents' original idea was that we would use canned milk, rather than bothering with a cow, but after one taste Penny and I absolutely refused to drink it, and threatened to back out of the entire enterprise. We could go live with one of our sets of grandparents, we said, while Mom and Dad could stay and do their thing out here in the woods. There were many times in the next two years when I thought back with regret that our parents had relented and agreed to get that cow.

In the long run, we didn't build a fence around a pasture, only around a small corral. Just put a bell on the cow and let her loose, Bill told us. She wouldn't go far, since there was a lot of good meadowland. It became the kids' chore to find the cow and drive her home in the evening for milking, but she learned that herself, since cows become uncomfortable when their udders fill with milk, so we usually found her plodding back toward the shed. When we picked up the cow, the woman we bought her from gave us lessons on how to milk her. Penny and I caught on right away, but Penny's hands were so small, she tired out before she got the job done, so for the first year, milking became my chore.

We bought the cow, but we didn't have to go looking for a cat. I was milking the cow one morning when I heard a demanding "meow!" behind me. There stood a huge orange and white cat, arching its back and rubbing against a post. It sounded hungry. I aimed a stream of milk in the direction of the cat, which promptly sat up on its haunches and gulped the milk as fast as I could squirt it. I told Mom about the cat, and being an animal lover, she opened a tin of tuna and sent me down to the cowshed with it. The cat materialized again, and when I put the dish down and moved away, he devoured the entire contents in one or two gulps, or so it seemed. The next time Dad went to town, Mom put cat food on the grocery list. Dad frowned at that, but I pointed out that we needed a cat to keep the mice out of the cow's grain, so he relented. It was several weeks before the cat let us touch him, but by the end of the summer, when the weather started to get cold, he had moved into the tent. We called him Mowser.

Carrying water was the chore I came to hate the most. We had chosen the building site because there was a spring across the road where water seeped from the hillside. Eventually, we would put in a pipe and have running water in the house, but that first summer, we carried all the water we used in buckets from the spring. Even after we had the pipe in, and buried deep enough not to freeze in the wintertime, we still had to carry water to the livestock after the creek froze in the winter. I learned from my physics lessons, that a gallon of water weighs seven and a half pounds, so a four-gallon bucket of water weighs thirty pounds. Penny could only carry half a bucket, but that meant twice as many trips, so I struggled back with full buckets of water when I was sent to the spring. After the spring was boarded up to make it easier to dip pails of water out of it, the surface became covered with algae. Grace Herman told us to put a frog in the spring to keep the water clean. The frog would eat the algae. Mom was horrified.

"Clean! With a slimy thing like a frog in it?"

"Frogs aren't slimy," Grace replied, looking in Penny's direction. "Are they, Penny?"

Penny shook her head. "No. They're neat. I kissed one to see if it would turn into a prince." She scowled. "It didn't."

"Anyway," Grace went on, "they eat the algae. Try it. You'll see."

Mom agreed reluctantly, but said she would boil the water for a while to make sure it was safe to drink. She had to abandon this idea after a day or two, when we realized that the boiled water could never be cooled down enough to be enjoyable to drink. Rather than drink the tepid water, Penny and I sneaked bottles of water dipped straight from the spring. We also caught Dad doing the same.

Penny and I went down to the creek with a small covered pail of water, caught a frog, and transported it to the spring. Occasionally while filling a bucket from the spring, we would scoop up the frog and would have to catch it and put it back. We thought the frog might be lonely and decided to give it a mate. Evidently we had selected a mate of the opposite sex, because our water was soon filled with tadpoles. We took the second frog out and returned it to the creek, but for a few days, we had to strain the tadpoles out before we used the water.

We soon learned how to identify, and avoid, thistles, nettles and poison ivy. We also discovered that it was no fun to go barefoot. The problem was porcupine quills. The day we arrived, Penny decided to take off her shoes and run around barefoot. She had only gone about three steps when she let out a shriek of pain and flopped down, holding her foot. A porcupine quill was sticking out of it. Mom examined the sole and since the quill didn't seem deeply embedded, tried to work it out. Penny let out another shriek. Bill Herman and Dad came running. Mom and Dad held a conference trying to decide what to do, but Bill went over to his pickup truck and came back with a pair of pliers.

"Stick your foot up here, honey," he said.

He held Penny's foot, grasped the quill close to the spot it entered the flesh, and yanked. The scream she let out that time made all the neighbour's cattle grazing in the meadow raise their heads in alarm. But almost immediately she stopped, realizing that her foot no longer hurt.

"Them quills have barbs like fishhooks only more so, so's they stick onto what they hit. Them porcupines walk real slow and can't outrun animals that prey on them, so they need some other means of defence. There's not many predators willing to tackle them. You gotta just jerk 'em out. But get as close as you can to the business end or you'll just break 'em off. Then you have to just let 'em fester out."

Mom looked a bit faint, I thought, but she pulled herself together and went for the first aid kit to get a Band-aid. Penny put her socks and shoes back on and tentatively stood up. Discovering that there was no longer any pain, she grinned at Bill and said, "Thank you, Mr. Herman."

Chapter Three

We didn't plant a garden that summer, although Mom had planned to. It turned out that Grace Herman was an avid gardener and grew enough stuff to feed an army. She always loaded us down with veggies, and Penny and I would do chores for her in exchange. Grace's chickens laid more eggs than the Hermans could use, so we also had a constant source of eggs, even though we had to overlook the occasional blood spot in the white of an egg.

The Hermans lived about a half a mile upstream from us. We had another neighbour about two hundred yards downstream. He was a man of about sixty with an ugly face and a perpetual scowl. His name was Stone, but Penny and I started calling him 'Old Stoneface.' We didn't like him and he wasn't too fond of children either.

The Hermans, on the other hand, were wonderful neighbours, always willing to lend a helping hand; or to send us home with a pan of fresh-baked rolls or a pail of strawberries from the garden.

Our third neighbour in the big meadow on the other side of the creek was a family named Monke. They ran cattle in the meadow and had lots of horses.

Because there were so many other things to do, it took several days to build the floor and framework for the larger, permanent tent. In the meantime, we slept in a tent we had used for camping.

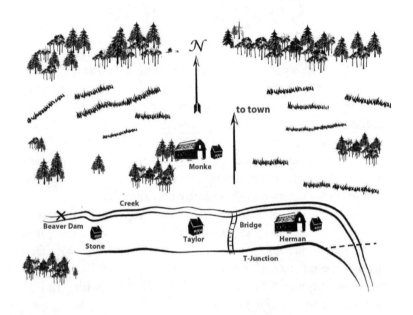

The third night we were there, it began to rain. We were awakened in the middle of the night by the appearance of puddles of water that had seeped up through the plastic floor of the tent and were soaking our sleeping bags. We spent the rest of the night huddled in the cab of our pickup.

Fortunately, the rain stopped during the day, so that we were able to get the tent and sleeping bags dried out. Thinking ourselves clever, we decided to put a tarp underneath the tent to keep the floor dry. That night, it rained again, and the wind came up and blew rain under the second tarp we had placed over the tent so that the water ran down the side and pooled on the tarp under the tent, again seeping up through the floor. Once again, we spent the remainder of the night huddled in the cab of our pickup.

To our great relief, the big tent was ready for us to move into the next night. It still needed a permanent roof built over it, but the rain had stopped and we slept that night without getting wet.

By the end of our first week at Beaver Creek, the big tent was covered by a board roof, we had moved our possessions into it, and we had set up the space to use it most efficiently. Well, not exactly. Mom did almost all the work, with my help. A kitchen stove we had found at a store in the nearest town had not yet been picked it up, so Mom was still cooking on a propane camp stove. When the weather turned hot after days of rain, the tent was like an oven, so we rolled up the sides to get air moving through to try to cool it off.

A few days after we moved to the valley, and the big tent was made ready to live in, Penny and I set out to explore the banks of the creek, not realizing that the rains had softened the banks. One crumbled beneath us and sent us sliding down the muddy bank into the creek up to our waists. We whooped with joy. Such fun! A water fight broke out. Half an hour later, the two of us, soaking wet and slathered with mud accumulated as a result of climbing back up the muddy bank, returned to the tent. Mom eyed us with horror. We changed into dry clothes and presented our dirty ones to Mom. She promptly sent us to the spring to lug enough water to at least wash out the mud. We had carried water earlier in the day, a chore we had come to hate. We rebelled at having to carry more water down from the spring.

"If you want clean clothes, you carry the water to wash them," Mom ordered.

"I don't care if they're clean. Just let the mud dry out," I replied.

"Well, I care. Go get the water."

"I can't," Penny said. "I hurt my arm."

"You didn't hurt your arm," I snarled. "You're just trying to get out of working."

"But it really hurts," she whined.

"No it doesn't."

"Yes it does."

"Shut up, both of you. Derek, go get the water. Penny, go to bed."

"I don't want to go to bed."

"If you're hurt, you need to rest. If you don't want to rest, you're not hurt that bad. Derek, get on your way. Now."

When Mom took that tone, I know she meant business. I took the bucket and trudged to the spring. I returned with the water.

"Rinse the mud off your jeans and do Penny's, too. Hang them on the line. At least, they should dry in this wind." I grudgingly complied.

Mom noticed me scratching my armpit. "What's the matter with you?" she demanded.

"I dunno." I took off my shirt and found a tick busily attaching itself to my skin. Mom took one look and complained loudly, "Ticks. That's all we need!" She took hold of the little beast right near the skin and pulled it off. She dropped it into my hand and told me to take it down to the privy and throw it in. When I got back, she ordered Penny and me to make a thorough search of our bodies for more of them.

Dad had gone into town to get the stove and pick up our mail. When he came home, he flopped on his bed saying, "I'm pooped. I'll put in the stove tomorrow."

Mom managed to light the propane stove on the fifth try. The matches had gotten damp in the high humidity of the rainy days. The steaks were half done and the canned veggies not yet heated when the wind came up. The sides of the tent were rolled up for ventilation, and the sudden wind roared through like a whirlwind and blew out the burners on the stove. Mom tried to re-light them, but couldn't find a dry enough match to do the job. She called out to Dad, but he was sound asleep, snoring peacefully. Mom prodded his limp body vigorously. Dad awoke with a start and asked when supper was going to be ready.

"Later," Mom snarled. Dad complained and Mom told him, "If you want supper right now, get it yourself."

"Now wait a minute Liz. I've been working hard and you've had all day to get things done. You should have supper ready."

Mom looked like a volcano about ready to erupt. "If you don't think *I've* been working, you should have stayed here and set up all this furniture yourself."

"Okay. Okay. When will supper be ready?"

"When I can find a dry match and get this damned stove lit."

"I think I've got some in the cab of the truck." Dad hurried out.

I felt remorseful. "I'm sorry, Mom. I'll try to help more."

She nodded her thanks, then passed the back of her hand over her sweaty face. "I never realized how much work living like this would be." She sighed. "This simple life is turning out to be murder."

It had not taken long for Mom to realize that we had probably gotten in over our heads in trying to live in the wilderness. Dad, however, would not condone this attitude, and we learned not to complain when he was around.

Chapter Four

To get to the meadow where we lived, we drove along the bank of a small river, eventually turning off of it and climbing to a low divide. The gravel road wound down through dense forest, and then came out about halfway along one side of the huge meadow. Just into the meadow was the sprawling collection of buildings of the Monke ranch. The road crossed the creek over a wooden bridge and ended at a T-junction. If you turned left, up the creek, you would pass the Hermans' place on the bank of the creek shortly before the road dived back into the woods and followed the creek up a canyon. If you turned right at the T-junction, you passed our building site and Stone's cabin, both of them between the road and the creek, which as it meandered through the meadow, ran sluggishly, with a few large pools where trout lurked.

We had enough money to buy the land when Dad received a large settlement on an accident claim back in Idaho. There was enough money left over to keep us going for a while. He also had a business that he could do anywhere, editing technical articles for people who knew how to do things but not how to write about them. Back in our old home, he did everything by e-mail. When we moved out here to the Beaver Valley, he made arrangements with the drug store in Arrow, the nearest town, to send and receive faxes. He also arranged with a lady in town to type letters for him if he had to reply to an incoming fax before his next trip to town. He did most of his work on a portable manual typewriter, not bothering with making carbon copies, because he could make photocopies on the drug store's copier. Sometimes he would take one of us into town with him. It was our one contact with civilization except for our occasional trips to Caribou.

After several days of hard labour to get our new home site into acceptable condition, and a few more days of rain, the sun came out and I found that I had some time to explore. First I headed down the creek to see what I could find down that way. Penny came running after me.
"Wait. I want to go with you."
I let out a sigh and gazed heavenward, preparing my usual responses when I didn't want to be burdened by a little sister tagging along. But then I realized that there were no other companions to spend time with and talk to, so maybe it would be okay to have someone—even my little sister—to share my adventure with me.
"Okay," I said grudgingly.
A short way beyond our home, the near bank of the creek turned out to be composed of a series of rock outcroppings separated by small gullies filled with vegetation. Small rivulets were now coursing down these gullies, though they would be completely dry come summer. Frequently we would have to climb over an outcropping and make our way down the next gully to get back to the creek. The vegetation in one turned out to be a sprawling blackberry bush. We did not identify it as such, since it was too early for berries and was in flower. We did learn that this bush had wicked thorns. We climbed back up the gully and crossed over another outcropping which led to a more level area where we could walk back to the creek. Here we found a fence that ran partway into the creek, and we could see the cabin of our neighbour we knew of only as Mr. Stone. He was not living

here at the time. We heard that he was a teacher and would come out to his cabin once school was over, another week yet.

We waded around the end of the fence and climbed up to the cabin. It was small, with only three or four rooms, we thought. There was no chimney or stovepipe, but along one side was a large propane tank. We tried to look in through the windows, but there were heavy curtains on all of them and we could not see anything. Another propane tank stood alongside a small building behind the cabin, which we figured was probably a workshop. Here again, the windows were curtained. It was also secured with a heavy padlock. We wondered what kind of work the man did there. Did he have a hobby he indulged in during the summer? We decided to come back for a visit when the man moved in.

The opposite bank of the creek was flat and covered with grass, so we decided to wade across the creek and go back home that way. The creek was swollen from the spring rains so we continued on down to try to find a place shallow enough to cross. What we found was a beaver lodge above a small beaver dam in the process of being built, which explained the deep pool we were following. Delighted we walked slowly toward it so as not to scare the beavers, and then lay down on our stomachs to watch them. In all the time we lived on Beaver Creek, we only occasionally actually saw the beavers at the lodge, though we saw them at work, but on this day we were in luck. Not only were the parent beavers working to mend some damage done to the dam by the swollen stream, but their babies were swimming around and playing in the water. We watched them for a long time, fascinated, until the adults finished their work and herded their young back into the lodge.

Downstream from the beaver lodge a tree had fallen across the creek. "Maybe we can walk across on that," I suggested.

When we arrived at the fallen tree, we realized that below it the creek was running more swiftly and was starting its descent into the canyon.

"I think we might fall off," Penny said doubtfully.

"I think we can walk across it. I've done things like that before," I bragged. "Do you want me to go first?"

"No. I'll go first. Then you can rescue me when I fall off."

She started across, but called out that the wet bark was slippery. She sat down straddling the log, and inched her way to the other side, getting up once to work her way around a branch that was sticking up. On the far side, she happily jumped off and shouted, "Your turn."

I wasn't about to show that I was afraid to walk the length of any stupid old tree. I started across boldly, not looking down at the water rushing underneath, but watching where I put each foot. At the midway point, over the deepest water, I stepped on a spot of loose bark, which abruptly slid off, sending me, with arms flailing to keep my balance, over the edge. I plunged into the muddy water, my feet finally reaching the bottom, only to discover that the creek bed was composed of mud. I floundered to the surface and started to swim, but the current was carrying me rapidly downstream. After what seemed like an age, but was probably no more than a minute, my feet struck solid rock as I reached an area of shallow rapids. I pulled myself to my feet and waded to the shore. Penny had run down the bank and was waiting, laughing her head off. She told me she had thought I was a goner and would be swept clear out to the ocean. Her laughter, she told me, was from relief, not mockery.

I plopped down on the bank to take off my shoes so I could pour the water out of them, but hastily jumped up again, brushing my hand across my backside, and then looking at the spot where I had sat down. I saw a nice green plant that was unfamiliar to me. I put my hand down to feel the fuzzy leaves and jerked it away. The leaves were really prickly. Later I learned that this was a thistle, another thing that stuck barbs into you if sat upon it or handled it. I knew what a fully grown thistle looked like, but didn't recognize the newly sprouted plant.

Living this simple life was turning out to be painful.

I stripped off my T-shirt, wrung the water out of it, and tucked it under my belt, feeling the sun on my bare back as we walked back up the creek. We decided to walk all the way to the bridge instead of trying to cross the creek again.

When we came abreast of our campsite, our parents and Bill Herman spotted us and started waving and calling to get our attention.

"Don't go any farther," Dad shouted. "Those bulls are dangerous."

"What?" I yelled back.

"The bulls," Dad replied, pointing toward the herd of cattle between us and the bridge.

"What about them?" I looked toward the cattle calmly grazing along the bank of the creek. One of the bulls was lumbering toward us, shaking his head, which held a pair of curved horns. He was snuffling through his nose as he stopped and eyed us.

It was Bill Herman who answered this time, with an urgent tone in his voice. "You don't want to tangle with them bulls. They'll get you on one of them horns and throw you right up in the air."

I looked back at the advancing bull. He stopped and began to paw the ground.

"Can you kids swim?" Bill asked.

"Sure. Why?"

"Then jump in the crick and swim across. It's safe here."

Penny started to laugh, and waved to the bull. "He looks nice," she called out.

It was Mom who took over. In a voice I had heard only twice before—when Penny was three and had started to run out into the street, and when I was small and Mom had seen a couple of unsavoury-looking men walking toward me—she called out, "Both of you. Jump in the creek and swim over here. Now!

I took one more look at the bull that was again advancing toward us, grabbed Penny by the hand and ran to the bank of the creek. We slid down the bank and into the water, swimming as swiftly as we could. I stayed behind Penny, keeping an eye on her and acting the part of big brother protecting little sister. She didn't need my help; she was sure as a fish in any kind of water. We pulled ourselves up the opposite bank. Penny turned to look back across the creek.

"Oh, he's going away," she said with obvious regret.

We got a thorough briefing from Bill Herman on what a range bull could do to us while protecting his herd.

Actually, I was kind of glad we'd swum across. Now I wouldn't have to explain why I came home soaking wet. But Penny promptly put paid to that, describing with exaggerated flailing motions, how I had fallen off the log. The adults had a good laugh, while I tried to think of ways to get even. But even then, Penny had the last laugh.

Mom sent us into the tent to change out of our wet clothes, forgetting for the moment that I was at the age where my body was changing. If I was deliberate about it, I could keep my voice in a lower register, but it occasionally escaped and shot upward. For years we had taken baths together and had no feeling of embarrassment at being naked together. But now my body was physically changing and I was not yet comfortable with it. There was no way out. Our tent was not divided into rooms. As I slipped off my underpants, I heard Penny giggle.

The creek attracted me on another day. I wanted to go fishing. Dad doesn't care about fishing, but Mom does, so on a day when she went into town, Mom got a licence for herself and one for me also. Penny could fish if she was with one of us, but her catch would count toward a licence holder's limit.

I set out for the creek with my new fishing rod and some earthworms I'd dug up. Penny, as usual, tagged along. On the other side of the creek, we could see one of the Monkes' dogs running toward us. This was the friendly dog. There was another dog that took his job as a watchdog seriously. I would eventually make friends with that one, but I had no trouble doing so with this dog. He came running over to the creek, hesitated, then jumped into the deep pool where I had planned to fish.

"I'll never catch anything here now," I grumbled, remembered being told that to disturb the water would scare the fish away. The wet dog lolloped over and shook himself vigorously, soaking both of us. Penny grabbed the rod from me, marched over to the creek, and flung the baited hook into the water. Immediately, the line went taut and began to reel out.

"Reel it in," I shouted. "Here, let me." Between us we landed a foot-long trout. We caught our limit of six trout in that pool and the next one down. We had trout for supper, one of many times in the summer months that we did so.

So much for the intelligence of fish, I thought uncharitably.

One time though, when we caught fish for supper, we didn't get to eat them. We laid them out on the picnic table, and went to do something else. When we came back we found nothing on the table but some fish heads, gills, and tails. And, oh yes, one large orange and white cat, licking his lips and smiling.

Chapter Five

Mom and Dad were down there by the creek the day we had the run-in with the bull, trying to figure out where a fence around a horse pasture should be. Penny and I had been bugging them about getting us horses. The promise of a horse for each of us had been the primary reason for our willingness to come out to this isolated place, and we had been very persistent in our demands.

The next morning they were down there again. I went along. We saw a stocky young man on a big bay horse riding slowly through the cattle. He came over and stopped across the creek from us.

"You the folks who bought this place?" he asked.

"We are. I'm Phil and this is Liz Taylor. This is our son, Derek."

"Hi. I'm Con Monke. My dad owns this land over here on this side. We run cattle on the meadow. Does your land go up to the bridge?"

"No, it goes mainly down toward Stone's place. We're figuring out where to put a pasture for horses. We promised the kids that they can have horses."

"You should just fence off this flat land here by the crick. Don't try to put a fence over that rocky stuff down there," Con said, waving an arm toward the Stone cabin. "There's no grass there anyway, and you'd have a hard time driving posts into that rock. This here is good grass and the earth's soft so you can drive metal posts in with no problem. We've got a post driver if you want to use it. A two strand bob-wire fence will keep horses in, if you tie some coloured strips along the top wire so's the horses can see it."

"Bob wire?" Mom muttered. "What's that? I thought we had to use rails."

"Barbed wire," I told her. I had worked for a vet the previous summer, walking dogs and cleaning cages in exchange for being allowed to ride his horses. Wire cuts were a common problem for the vet, because many horse owners used barbed wire even around horse pastures.

Dad and Con Monke were still discussing where to put the fence. Penny came running down to the creek and called out, "What's your horse's name."

"I call him Buck."

"Oh. Does he buck?"

"No, he don't. All our horses are well trained. We can't have any rogue ones."

"I want a horse."

"Yeah, that's what your dad said. Do you know how to ride a horse?"

"Sure. I ride a lot."

Dad laughed. "This kid will get on anything with four legs. She once got bucked off a sheep."

"It didn't have anything to grab hold of. It had been sheared."

Con laughed, relaxing in the saddle as if ready to stay a while. He looked at me. "How about you?"

"I used to do some work for a vet who also raised quarter horses. He let me ride them."

"Well, if you want to buy some horses, see my dad. We have lots and Dad always has some to sell. They'll be good horses too, and they're bomb-proof."

"They're *what*?" Dad asked.

"They don't get scared and shy at nothing, and they don't panic if someone waves something in their face."

"Oh."

"Dad will want to let you ride one before he lets you buy it. He don't want the horses ruined by someone who don't know how to handle them or wants to make them into a pet. They're good horses, and he don't want them ruined."

"We know how to handle horses," I said.

"Do you ride Western? 'Cause these horses ain't used to that English stuff."

"Sure. I always have."

"Well, see my Dad. Our cattle sometimes go across the crick up near the bridge where it's shallow. They won't go through your fence though. But keep clear of them bulls. They're mean when the cows are in season. They won't bother no one on horseback, though." Con rode away to continue checking on the cattle.

"What did he mean when he said that about the cows being in season?" Penny wanted to know.

"Never mind," Dad said brusquely.

"I'll tell you later," was Mom's response.

With Bill Herman's help and the Monkes' post driver and wire stretcher, the fence went up in a hurry. I took my turn driving the posts, and by the end of the day, my shoulders were so sore, I could hardly lift my arms. But I could lift them well enough to wolf down my supper.

Chapter Six

It was Friday evening of the last week in June, a time when schools were out for the year. Late in the evening, when it was still light, our other neighbour stopped by on his way to open his cabin. Mom and Dad walked out to meet him. The man, who appeared to be in his sixties, introduced himself only as Stone. Dad seemed to be happy to have another man to talk to, especially when he discovered that Stone was an ardent environmentalist. Dad was a person who turned up at protests and joined sit-ins in favour of environmental projects.

"We moved out here to be able to live with nature," Dad told Stone. "We think that this lifestyle will be good for the kids. They need to learn to be self-sufficient and not rely on all these new technical gadgets. Those things aren't needed for comfortable living. There's no electricity out here, or phones either, and we're in a dead space as far as cell phones are concerned."

"This suits me just fine, too," Stone replied. "I'm very happy to get away from pesky phones ringing all the time. All through the school year there are constant phone calls and e-mails to answer. Out here I can get away from all that noise. That's why I moved out here for my summers."

"What do you do for water? We have a spring just above the road. That's why we bought here. But you live on a rocky outcrop. Did you sink a well?"

"No, I bring water out in big jugs and use it sparingly. My cabin is right down by the creek, so I can wash clothes in water from the creek, and I can bathe in it. I only use the bottled water for food and drink."

"How do you heat your cabin?" Dad must have noticed the lack of a chimney or stovepipe.

"I don't. I'm only here two months in the summer. If it get cold and rainy, I just put on heavier clothes."

"I'm trying to teach our kids that they have to be careful what they use, because they can't just run to the store to get something if we run out."

"You have kids then?"

"Yes," Mom answered. "We have two; Derek and Penny."

"Well, I don't like kids, so keep them away from my place."

I could see the scowl still on Mom's face when I went with her back to the tent. "That attitude seems odd for a man who teaches school," she said.

I had a different reason for objecting to an opinion Dad expressed in that conversation. Dad had said we didn't need modern technology to live comfortably and that was why we moved out here to Beaver Creek. That was definitely not my opinion of life out here, and comfortable was not the word I would have used to describe our lifestyle. Nor did I think the lack of technology was something to be happy about. My view was quite the opposite. A neighbour of ours back where we used to live in Idaho, an elderly lady who had lived in conditions more primitive than ours, said that when World War II was over and new things began to be available to nearly everyone, she and many others moved to towns and cities and began to enjoy life. I was already beginning to regret our move out here to lead such a primitive life.

Dad and Stone talked for a while longer, mainly about the environment. Before Stone left, he brought a newspaper from his SUV and showed Dad a story in it, leaving the paper with Dad. It was something about oil pipelines, I learned when I read the paper the next day. A short while later, we saw lights go on, first in Stone's workshop, and then in the cabin, obviously from propane lanterns like the ones we used.

I said to Penny, "I guess we'd better stay away from him."

But Penny had a different idea. "We ought to go down there and meet him and show him we're really nice kids and want to be friends."

"Yeah, maybe so. Let's wait a few days, though."

Anyway, Mom had another plan for us. "Remember what Con Monke said about putting coloured strips on the top wire? Well, I've got an old yellow-green T-shirt I never wear. We can cut it up and you kids can tie the strips on the fence.

While I helped the next morning to build the gate for our new pasture, Penny tied on the strips. There wasn't enough cloth to finish the job, but it would have to do until we went to town and got some more fabric. Our pasture was now ready for the horses. The cow could use it, too, or she could still just be turned loose. Later, we would buy hay and grain to feed the animals during the winter.

Now, it was time to get our horses.

Chapter Seven

Dad drove us over to the Monke ranch and Abe Monke, a big, barrel-chested man, led us to a corral filled with horses of every colour. They were almost all of the sturdy quarter horse type, the typical cowpony. The exception was a smaller mare, solid bay in colour. Monke put a halter on her and led her over.

"This here little horse has raised all my kids. She's gentle and real nice to ride. She'd be nice for the little girl."

I could see storm clouds on Penny's face. She did not like being called a little girl. She stepped forward, pulled a carrot from a pocket, placed it on the palm of her hand and held out her hand, palm up. The bay mare manipulated the carrot with her soft muzzle and then picked it gently off Penny's hand. Penny patted her on the neck and rubbed behind her ear. The mare searched for more carrots, but finding none, stood calmly for Penny to continue petting her. When Monke noticed the way Penny offer the carrot to the horse, I saw him nod his approval.

"What's her name?" Penny asked.

"Peanuts."

"Can I ride her?"

"Sure. I'll throw a saddle on her." He led the mare into the barn, took a youth's saddle off a rack and saddled Peanuts, shortening the stirrup leathers to the length he thought would be right for Penny. "If you buy this horse," he said to Dad, "I'll sell this saddle to you too. My kids has outgrown it. But when this girl outgrows it, I'd like to buy it back. I'll have grandkids who'll need it then. I'll throw the saddle blanket and bridle in for good measure."

I had the feeling that Dad ought to bargain pretty hard with this guy when it came to price. I wondered if Dad had checked on the cost of second hand saddles. I think he had just looked up the prices people were paying for horses.

Monke led the mare to a ring used to exercise the horses. "Do you need help getting on?" he asked Penny.

"Nope. I can do it."

She grasped the horn and cantle of the saddle, and jumped up, neatly placing her foot in the stirrup and swinging on. Gathering the reins, she kicked the mare into motion and rode confidently around the ring at an easy trot. She pulled up in front of Dad. "Can I have this horse please, Dad?"

Dad turned toward Monke. "I think you've made a sale."

"You couldn't do better."

We left Penny to ride around the ring and went back to the corral. I noticed a boy sitting on the top rail. He looked like he was in the middle-teen years of age, but was short and skinny. He watched silently while we looked over the horses. Monke walked over to a big pinto horse, white with brown spots, and put a halter on him, leading him over to us. "This here's a beautiful horse, and he's nice to ride."

I heard the boy sitting on the fence call out softly, "Hey, kid." I turned toward him. "Don't buy that one," he said. "That's a pack horse. You can ride him, but he just plods. Get Dad to show you that chestnut over there, the one with the big blaze." He pointed toward the horse. I nodded and walked over to where Monke was showing Dad the pinto.

"Mr. Monke, I'd like to look at that chestnut—that one with the blaze."

"Sure." Monke slipped the halter off the pinto, walked through the herd of horses, and led the chestnut out. I also had a carrot, and I pulled it out of my shirt pocket, handing it to the horse the way Penny had done. The chestnut took the carrot off my hand. The soft muzzle whiffled around over my hand, looking for another, then having seen where the carrot had come from, began exploring my shirt with his soft nose. "I'd like to ride him. What's he called?"

Monke looked over toward the boy sitting on the fence. "Whatdaya call this one?"

"Blaze."

"Chad here, he's my youngest son. What's your name?"

"Derek."

Chad slid down from the fence, walked over and offered his hand, "Hi Derek."

I shook hands. "Hi."

We went over to the ring, where Penny was still happily riding. Monke brought out a well-used, rough-side-out roping saddle and flung it onto the chestnut. "These stirrups oughta fit you. You're pretty tall." After slipping the halter off and replacing it with a bridle, he handed me the reins, and I swung aboard. Blaze responded to my gentle pressure of heels on his sides and to the twitch of the reins to turn him toward the centre of the ring. I rode for several minutes, putting him through his paces, making him turn, back, and pivot. I came back with a grin on my face. "I like him."

We went into the house, and while Dad and Monke dickered over prices, Chad led Penny and me into the kitchen. Mrs. Monke looked up, smiling shyly as Chad introduced us as "My new friend, Derek—and his sister."

"I'm Penny." My sister didn't want to be left out.

"Hello Derek and Penny," Mrs. Monke said. "I'm glad you moved out here. Chad never had no one to hang out with in the summer before now. You'll stay for lunch, won't you?"

"Mom's a great cook. Stay," Chad said.

"I'll go ask Dad." Penny ran out and quickly returned with the positive answer.

Mrs. Monke served us huge bowls of chili and emptied a pan of freshly baked biscuits onto a plate. "Eat all you want. There's lots more."

Looking at Mrs. Monke, I could see why Chad was a shrimp of a kid while his brother was tall and heavy-set. Con took after his big burly dad and Chad after his mom who couldn't have been more that five feet tall or weighed more than a hundred pounds. There was quite a spread between the two sons' ages as well. I asked, "Do you have any other kids?"

"Conner is my oldest. You met him. I have a daughter. She's seventeen now, but she left home 'cause she didn't have no one to hang out with summers. The kids go out to school and come home for Christmas and summers. Darlene left and went to live with her boyfriend's family. They was too young to get married then. They're hitched now, but Darlene had her first baby before, and another's on its way. So we'll have grandkids coming out here before long." She looked pleased about that. I figured it must be lonely out here for her as well.

The men came into the kitchen and sat down to eat. They both looked happy.

"Derek, I bought you the saddle you were using. I hope that's okay with you."

"Sure. Thanks, Dad." Actually, I liked the idea. It would make me look like a real cowboy when I rode my new horse, using the battered old saddle. After lunch Penny and I mounted our new steeds again, turned out onto the road, and cantered home, Dad following behind us in the truck. Mom came out to greet us, and to be introduced to Peanuts and

Blaze. She brought more carrots, and that went over well with the ponies.

"We had lunch at the Monkes', so can we go out and ride?" I asked.

"All right, but stay close."

We rode to the Hermans' home and showed them our mounts, before heading down the other way past Stone's cabin. We rode to where the road descended into a canyon, where we turned back, rode home, unsaddled our horses, and turned them out into their new pasture. They trotted around the fence, exploring their new home, then settled down to graze.

Chapter Eight

Early the next evening, Chad came by, riding the same bay horse his brother, Conner, had been riding a few days earlier.

"Why don't you saddle up and I'll show you some good places to ride."

"Okay, sounds good." I whistled to Blaze and to my surprise, he came running. Probably because last night, I'd had a bucket of oats in my hand when I whistled. I saddled him, pausing to shorten the stirrup leathers one notch. They had been a little too long yesterday.

While I was saddling my new horse, Blaze, Chad pulled a small round tin out of the rear pocket of his jeans, took the lid off, and removed a small amount of a dark brown substance that he placed in his mouth between his lower lip and gums. He offered the can to me. "Wanna try some?"

"What is it?"

"Smokeless tobacco. You can't smoke out here. If you drop a match in the grass once it gets dry, you'd start a forest fire. Or if you drop cigarette ash in the barn, you could burn it down. We use this stuff instead. Try some."

I shook my head. "I'm not old enough to use tobacco products."

"It won't hurt you none. You don't breath it in, so it can't cause cancer in your lungs."

"Well, I still don't think I should." I knew Mom would have a fit if she knew. I wasn't willing, however, to use parental disapproval as an excuse when talking to this boy. I wanted to be his friend, and I didn't want him laughing at me.

We set off down the road, past Stone's cabin, and into the canyon, riding down the steep grade to the bottom where Beaver Creek emptied into a larger stream, Jewel Creek. Chad pointed to a trail leading up the larger creek. "If you go up thataway, there are all kinds of good trails up there. You can go all the way to the US border."

"Do you ever ride across it?"

"Can't. There's a fence. There ain't much up ahead. This road climbs up out of the canyon and there ain't no trails off it."

"Where does the road go from here?"

"It goes over the ridge and then down into the river canyon. There's another town there where this here crick runs into the river. It's even smaller than Arrow." Arrow is the town where we got our mail and groceries.

We rode back to the meadow, and as we passed Stone's cabin, Chad said, "Stay away from that guy. He don't like kids and he don't like no one hanging around his place."

Seeing the tall, sturdy fence around Stone's cabin, I asked," Does he have dogs?"

"Naw. He don't like our dogs neither."

"Then why does he have this high fence?"

"That's to keep our cattle out. He don't need that kind of fence to stop the cattle, but that's what he says."

After supper, I asked Mom if I could use smokeless tobacco. Her answer was an emphatic "No!"

"Why not? It's not harmful, because you don't inhale anything."

"Who told you that?"

"Chad did. He uses it."

"He does, does he? I wonder whether his parents know."

"They must. You can tell that he uses it, because you can see where he carries the container." I had noticed the small white ring on the hip pockets of blue jeans, where the indigo dye had been worn off, caused by the circular can the tobacco came in. I'd seen a number of cowboys at the quarter horse farm where I used to work and ride, many with that tell-tale ring on the hip pockets of their Wranglers.

"I don't care. The answer is no. I don't want to hear anything more about it."

"Can I carry an empty can in my pocket?"

"No!"

Even then, I had a vague feeling in the back of my mind that something was wrong with Chad's reasoning about the lack of danger from using smokeless tobacco. It dawned on me that if tobacco smoke could cause cancer in one's lungs, the other form of tobacco could cause cancer in one's mouth.

I thought Mom was being unreasonable about not allowing me to carry an empty tobacco tin in my pocket. I eventually got the better of the argument, however, though not from anything I said. I was growing rapidly and needed new clothes, especially jeans, as the ones I had been wearing barely reached the tops of my ankles now. Penny, who had brought only cotton slacks and shorts, also need the tough western jeans, especially if she was going to be doing any serious riding.

Mom heard that the town of Arrow, where we got our mail and our groceries, was having a community yard sale. We all piled into the truck and went into town to see if we could be outfitted in new duds without breaking the bank. I wandered over to a table filled with used jeans of every size. I found a pair of Levis in one size larger and longer than those I was wearing. I picked them up and went on rummaging through the pile. Right at the bottom was a pair of faded Wranglers, the typical cowboy jeans, with the identifying W stitched in orange on the hip pockets. It had the characteristic ring at the bottom of the right hip pocket. I folded the jeans so that the pocket wouldn't show and presented them to Mom at the cashier's table. Mom didn't realize what I had done until the first time I wore them, and by then it was too late for her to veto my choice.

While we were in Arrow, Penny and I got permission to stroll around the town and investigate what it had to offer. It was a small town, no more than one thousand in population. It had the usual stores and a café with surprisingly good food. We had lunch there after we had reconnoitred the town. Surprisingly, in these days when pay phones are nearly a thing of the past, Arrow had three of them; one at the general store, one at the café, and another at the gas station. We learned that Arrow, like the Beaver Valley, had no cell phone access, only land lines, hence the pay phones.

But what interested us most was the veterinary clinic. Adjacent to the road leading to the border crossing, the clinic had a sign reminding travellers that any pets they had with them would require a rabies vaccination in order to cross the border. We saw pens for dogs to exercise in and saw a sleek black Labrador in one of them. The dog came over to the fence, wagging his tail. We couldn't pet him because of the double chain-link fence around the pens. A teenage girl was hosing down the other pens, and seeing us, came over to talk.

"That dog belongs to the Mounties. His name is Jet, and his handler lives here in town. He's a drug-sniffing dog. The cop takes him down to the border crossing, and he sniffs all the cars and catches people trying to smuggle drugs across.

I can tell you don't have any pot on you or he'd be barking his head off."

"Why's he here at the vet's," Penny asked.

"This part is the boarding kennel. It's separate from the clinic, so the boarders won't get any diseases from the sick animals."

"Oh. Good idea."

"I'd like to have a dog like that," I said wistfully.

We chatted a little while longer, then the girl went back to work and we went on our way.

Arrow was down in a valley with walls so steep that by midafternoon the sun went down behind a cliff. I thought I wouldn't like to live there; I liked more open spaces. The vet clinic was set against the base of a high cliff of solid rock. We could see trees hanging on precariously to the top of it.

Back at the yard sale, I spotted a table holding books as well as a pile of old maps. I looked through the maps and discovered that they were out-dated aeronautical charts that not only showed the location of towns and cities, highways and railroads, of provincial and international borders, and of tall structures and terrain features, but are topographical maps as well. I paid twenty-five cents for the whole stack.

Finding a picnic table in the park where the sale was being held, I spread out the chart for the area of British Columbia where we resided. I found Arrow on the chart, and knowing that Beaver Creek where it traversed the big meadow was west of the town, I found what looked to be it, just over the cliff to the west. I couldn't believe it! Finding a scale on one border of the map, I tried to figure out how far, as the crow flies, we were from our new home. I was just getting used to thinking in kilometres instead of miles. I knew that it was nineteen kilometres from the T-junction near our home to Arrow. On the way over, though the signs gave distances in kilometres, I had worked out in my head that we had driven about twelve miles to get to Arrow. I was relieved to see that on these charts the type of measurement was in miles—but they were nautical miles. What was a nautical mile? I dredged up from my memory the figure 1.15. But was the nautical mile longer or shorter than the mile I was used to, which I remembered was called a statute mile? Longer, I thought. I used a piece of paper I caught as it floated by on the breeze to mark the distance from the T-junction near our tent to the town of Arrow. Three nautical miles. In other words, about three and a half statute miles. And we had driven twelve miles to get here.

As I studied the map further, the reason for the extra distance was apparent. The ridge of which this high cliff was a part extended several miles to the north. We had to go around the north end of it.

The next time I rode with Chad, I suggested that we go east toward the cliff overlooking the town. "Maybe we can ride right up to the cliff and look over," I mused.

"Naw. We don't wanna go that way," Chad responded dismissively. "There's nothing up there, only clear-cuts.

I still thought I'd like to see for myself, but I had probably better go on my own and not with Chad. Something in his tone of voice told me that Chad really didn't want to ride in that direction. Maybe there was something that scared him up there.

As it turned out, we actually did get scared on one of Chad's favourite trails. We rounded a curve in the trail and found ourselves face to face with a big black bear.

I was riding in front at that point; the trails in the woods were not wide enough to ride side by side. Chad was right behind me. Both of our horses threw up their heads and snorted. They stopped dead in their tracks, and tried to wheel around and run back down the trail. I firmly reined Blaze in the direction we were going, not because I wanted to confront the bear, but because I did not want Blaze to get the idea he could do what he pleased. I wanted him to know that I was the one who gave the orders and would decide on the way to go. I made him stand for a moment, which I felt was safe enough since the bear had also stopped in its tracks and was eyeing us, but not showing aggression. I then calmly reined Blaze around and kept him from breaking into a run. As we trotted down the trail, I looked over my shoulder. The bear was lumbering back the way it had come. It was probably as scared of us as we were of it.

Keeping a tight rein on our horses, we rode back to Jewel Creek and found another trail going in a different direction. Chad pulled up beside me.

Hey, you really can handle a horse." This was high praise from a boy who was really cocky about his own ability to make horses do what he wanted. "Good thing that bear didn't have no cubs, or she would of charged us."

"If she had, I would have let Blaze run for his life," I replied chuckling.

"Yeah. Me, too. Did ya ever see a cougar?"

"No. Are there any in this area?"

"Yeah. I saw one once, out behind our barn. Scared me silly. I could've won the Olympics, I run so fast back to the house."

Bulls, bears, cougars. I wondered what other hazards there were out here.

Chapter Nine

One day, Penny said, "Let's go visit Old Stoneface. Maybe if he gets to know us he'll think we're okay."

I doubted it, but agreed to go.

Mr. Stone is a large man with an ugly face. His face looks as if it were made from leftovers. He scowls constantly. The guy can't help what he looks like, but he can help how he interacts with other people. Dad gets along with him, but Mom makes herself scarce whenever Old Stoneface, as Penny and I call him, stops by.

We walked down the road and stopped at Stone's gate. I was hoping he'd be in his workshop so I could see inside. He wasn't. He was in his house. The front door was open, but we couldn't see him, so I knocked loudly on the door. He came from the back of the house, and seeing us, angrily demanded that we leave.

Penny said politely, "We want to be friends. We're good kids."

"Well I don't want to be friends. Get going. And latch the gate. Don't leave it open."

Penny wanted to talk to him some more, but I took her arm as I told Stone, "We're just leaving, sir. We'll latch the gate." I pulled Penny along after me. Stone glowered after us until we were out on the road, walking away. Then he slammed his door shut.

So much for our goodwill efforts.

That evening, Stone came to our tent. Mom was inside washing up after dinner, with Penny's help. We had to take turns at kitchen duty. Back when we lived in a house, that involved clearing the table and stacking the dishes in the dishwasher. Here we had to clear the table and do the dishes by hand in a pan of water heated on the stove. We grumbled about this onerous chore, but Mom was firm. She didn't want to wash the dishes any more than we did I'm sure, and Dad refused absolutely to do what he carefully refrained from calling 'women's work.' He'd called it that once and he still bore the scars of Mom's anger.

Dad met Stone and invited him to have a seat at the picnic table we used when it was too hot to eat inside the tent. Stone got right down to his grievance.

"Your kids were on my property today. I told you to keep them away from my place. I don't want kids hanging around. I thought I made that clear when I first met you."

Dad turned to me. "Were you down at Mr. Stone's cabin today?"

I nodded. "Yes, we were. We just wanted to be friendly and let Mr. Stone know that we're good kids and won't do anything to damage his property. And we wouldn't steal anything."

"My children *are* good kids and can be trusted to respect other people's property," Dad answered earnestly.

"I don't care. I don't want them around." He glared at me. "Is that understood?"

"Yes, sir," I replied meekly.

Stone turned his back on me and then acted as if I wasn't there. I didn't slink away as he might have expected or hoped. I stood my ground as a person in my own right who deserved to be there. There was some general talk between Stone and my father, that Stone eventually steered toward the subject of the environment. Dad's ears pricked up, so to speak. That's his pet subject. He can get really riled up about threats to the environment. He's been on committees, attended rallies, and protested against things he thinks are doing damage to the planet. He seemed to be delighted to find someone to talk to about it.

"What do you think of these proposed pipelines that would take natural gas and oil to the west coast to be loaded onto tankers?" Dad asked.

"Pipelines," Stone thundered. "Don't ask me what I think about pipelines. They're the work of the devil. They tear up the land, and destroy wildlife habitat. And there will inevitably be tankers that run aground and spill huge quantities of oil into the ocean, killing fish and birds."

I saw Dad grin with joy. Here was someone who mirrored his own obsession. They talked for half an hour, laying out their views. There was no one to contradict them. They were having a ball. It was a bit boring to me, but suddenly the atmosphere changed.

"The people who run those companies are as good as murderers," Stone shouted, banging his fist on the table to emphasize his point. I winced; his vehemence startled me. "Those men should be shot! Even that would be too easy on them. They should be drawn and quartered."

"Now wait a minute," Dad almost stuttered, he was so alarmed. "They may be mistaken, but those men are only doing their job."

"They should know that their job kills living creatures."

"Maybe it does, but you can't just go around killing people because you don't like what they're doing. Besides, someone else would just take their place. I think the only way to counteract them is by education, by showing that there are other ways to live that don't cause so much damage."

"Education," Stone jeered. "When does anyone pay any attention to do-gooders who want to educate them?"

"You're a teacher, aren't you?" Dad countered.

Suddenly, Stone was laughing. "Oh, touché. You got me there, Taylor."

They parted on good terms, and except for a glare in my direction, Stone appeared to have forgotten the gripe he'd come over to our place to complain about.

After Stone had left, I asked Dad, "What did he mean by saying those men should be drawn and quartered?"

"He wanted to see them suffer."

"I get that, but what is it actually?"

"Oh, I see what you mean. It's a medieval form of execution where all the victim's arms and legs attached to horses and are pulled in different directions so the body is pulled apart."

"When they're alive?"

"Yes, when they are alive and conscious."

I shivered. "Oh! Sorry I asked."

Dad clapped me on the shoulder. "Well, don't have nightmares about it, son. It isn't done any more."

Late in August we went to Caribou to buy winter clothes, to get our dental check-up (that's when the dentist showed me pictures of cancer caused by chewing tobacco), and to talk to the program coordinator of the local schools. We also picked up the textbooks and other material we would need for the coming school year. Stone had described himself as a teacher, so Mom asked the lady whether Stone taught at a school in Caribou.

"Is that Casimir Stone you're asking about?"

"I don't know his first name," Mom told her.

"Big man with white hair and eyebrows that look like Niagara Falls? Scowls a lot?"

"Yes, that's him."

"He does teach science at the local high school. He used to be a chemistry professor at a major university. I don't remember which one, though."

"Why did he leave a university to teach in a high school?"

"I don't know. I wasn't here when he came, and he is sort of stand-offish, so it's hard to get to know him."

Mom frowned. "The reason I asked was that he told us he didn't like kids and not to let ours bother him. They went to his cabin once to try to get to know him and be friendly, but he chased them away. I think it's odd that a man who hates children would be a teacher."

"His students here seem to like his classes. That is, the ones who do their work do. He doesn't suffer fools or lazy students, though."

I asked, "Does he have some hobby that he works on a lot?"

"I don't know. Why do you ask?"

"Because he has a workshop that he keeps all locked up, and I wondered if he was working on something and didn't want anyone messing with it."

"I suppose he could, but as I said, he doesn't talk about himself very much."

On our way home Penny and I laughed about Stone's funny first name, rolling it off our tongues with exaggerated drawing out of the final r."

"Shut up," Dad yelled. "There is nothing funny about his name."

Mom joined in. "Actually Casimir is an old-fashioned name that isn't used very much these days. But it's a perfectly legitimate name, and you shouldn't make fun of him because of the name his parents gave him."

"Sorry, Mom," I mumbled.

Old Stoneface would stop by to talk to Dad from time to time, and once when the man had been away for several days, he brought us a *Globe and Mail* on his return. Compared with the local paper, which Dad would pick up every time he went to town, the *Globe and Mail* was a bonanza. Mom and Dad read it through from front to back, and I would read some of the articles, especially if they were about science. It was always the weekend edition, so there was a lot to read. Dad, however, grumbled about it, just as he did about the local paper.

"I'd just as soon not know the news. It's always the same; the war in Afghanistan; trouble between Israel and Palestine; some politician has gotten himself in trouble over what he said; the economy is headed for a recession because of some problem in the States about mortgages; some group is complaining about taxes; someone got another letter bomb in the mail; some girl disappeared when hitch-hiking along a highway in northern BC. I'd just as soon stay out here and let the rest of the world worry about troubles of their own making."

"It was nice of Mr. Stone to bring the paper, though," Mom murmured.

"I'll grant that. He should be leaving pretty soon to go back to Caribou, unless he's retired from teaching. I'll miss talking to him."

Stoneface did leave the next weekend. It was Labour Day weekend, and school started on Tuesday. Life threatened to get a bit more boring with Stoneface gone. I didn't like him, but he sure livened things up around here. But I had a thought in the back of my mind that I'd like to get into his workshop if I ever had a chance. I had the impression that Old Stoneface was more bothered by people hanging around his workshop than coming to his house, and I was dying to know what he was doing in there. Chad figured that Old Stoneface kept all his girly pictures there, and didn't want to be arrested for having porn in his house. I kept trying to think of ways to get in, but couldn't come up with any. It would have to wait until next summer.

Chapter Ten

On Saturday of the Labour Day weekend, Chad stopped by to shoot the breeze. I was busy with chores and told him I couldn't go riding right then. He stuck around for a while, and then asked, "Hey, Derek. Wanna go for a ride in the moonlight tonight?"

"Sure! Sounds great."

Our parents were going to pick up Chad's, and the two couples would drive into town to attend the Saturday night dance at the community hall, leaving us boys at home. Penny would go with them. There was an event at the local school for kids her age, and she had been invited. I wasn't interested in going to the dance because Mrs. Monke told me there wouldn't be anyone my age, and I figured I'd probably be bored.

I was supposed to stay home and go to bed at a decent hour, but the prospect of getting out from under the parental thumb for once appealed to fourteen-year-old me. I readily agreed. I was pretty certain that my folks wouldn't approve if I told them what I really planned to do, so I kept it to myself.

There was another reason for my eagerness for saddling up my horse and going for a ride in the moonlight. The night before, the bright moonlight had kept me awake and I sat on the sloping hillside below the tent looking out over the meadow, bathed in brilliant light of the nearly full moon. I had watched the cattle settle down for the night, a group of deer graze across the meadow, heard an owl with its plaintive hoot, and saw a coyote stalk one of the fawns before the deer sensed its presence and dashed away. Getting sleepy, I had been about to end my vigil and climb into bed, when I heard the clop of horses' hooves and the jingle of bits. Curious, I stayed and watched Chad's older brother, Conner, returning home with his pack string along the road that branched off at the T-junction. The horses stirred up dust from the unpaved road, forming a low cloud of dust that obscured their feet and made them look as if they were gliding on air.

I could recognize Conner by his usual slouch in the saddle, riding his big bay horse, leading another saddle horse and two packhorses. The last horse in the string was the pinto Monke had tried to sell to us for me to ride. It's white rump shone in the moonlight. The horses clattered across the wooden bridge over the creek, now appearing to have feet like they should, breaking the spell. I stretched, yawned, and headed for bed.

The memory was sufficient in itself to make a moonlight ride sound attractive.

Chad rode up while I was still saddling my horse. He swung a leg over his saddle horn, relaxing in the saddle, and pulled a can of smokeless tobacco out of his hip pocket, talking a pinch of the stuff and putting it inside his lower lip. He offered me some, but I shook my head. After having seen the dentist's pictures, just the sight of the tobacco turned my stomach.

"Hey! I know where there's pot being grown. I followed Con one day and found out where he gets it. C'mon. Let's ride over there and I'll show you."

I was startled. I'd never tried the stuff, and the warnings kids got from parents, teachers, and other people had scared me away from trying it. I guess I should thank my parents for teaching me respect for authority.

"No, I don't want to do that! It's against the law."

"Oh, don't worry. We're not going to get any. I just thought you'd like to know."

"Know what?"

"Where it's at! Then you never have to find someone to supply it to you. I know those guys who grow it, but they don't know I know. Con don't let me have any." The way Chad said this made it sound like a long-time grievance. "Let's just go look."

We didn't go by the road. Instead, Chad led off through the timber above the road, picking up a game trail. When I asked where we were going, he said, "Don't worry. I know my way all over these hills." We rode in silence for a while before Chad spoke again. "If you ever get lost around here, just give old Blaze his head and he'll take you home. These horses know where the barn is at. They don't never get lost."

The trail took us through dense forest alternating with open patches where the moonlight was so bright, you could read a book by it. Our eyes had to keep adjusting to the change from dark to light and back again. On occasion, we would come out on a bare area where we could see a portion of the valley below us. Nothing was moving, but we could occasionally hear a cow moo or a calf bleat. We heard the hoot of an owl somewhere in the trees that seemed to follow us for a ways.

We crossed the ridge separating the meadow from the upper reaches of Beaver Creek where it came down out of the mountains. When we rode down the other side of the ridge on an old logging road, unused for years, I recognized the area below us. I had gone fishing there with Mom a couple of times. The creek curved around away from the road and there was a brushy flat between it and the road. The logging road stopped abruptly where the new road along the creek had cut across it, and a steep bank dropped down to the gravel road that followed the creek. We stopped our horses when we came to this steep bank.

The hillside was bathed in moonlight, but the canyon floor was as dark as the bottom of a well. Only vague outlines of the creek and the gravel road that ran along the near side were visible.

At the upper end of this brushy flat, where the creek re-joined the road, a small cabin had recently been built. We could see a light on in the cabin, shining through the open door. I knew that two men who claimed to be working a mining claim lived there.

Chad's mood changed. "Let's tie our horses up and sneak down there. I don't see no one around."

"What are you planning on doing?"

"They grow it down there on that flat. The brush hides it."

"Do they do any mining? It's a claim, isn't it?"

Chad gave a snort. "Mining, hell! There's no gold around here. C'mon."

We rode back up the logging road a short ways, tied our horses among some trees, and made our way down the old logging road on foot. We could see the cabin at the upper end of the flat, its open door spilling out light, with two men sitting on the doorstep drinking beer. The sound of their voices came to us, but we couldn't make out the words.

"They can't see us once we get down on the road. C'mon."

The main road up the canyon followed the near slope of the hill, the meadow being on the other side. We slid down the bank above the road, and ran across it into a grove of trees at the lower end of the brushy area. We could no longer see nor hear the men at the cabin, but there was no indication that we had been spotted either. Chad led the way along the edge of the grove until we reached an expanse of grass that separated it from the thick brush covering most of the flat. The grove of trees we had been moving through was in shadow, but the moonlight had now touched the valley floor. Chad signaled me to follow him across the open space, now as bright as day in the light of the full moon.

At the edge of the brush, Chad crouched and motioned me to do the same.

"There'll be some brush to hide the plants, but there should be some right in there."

"Chad, let's go back. I don't like this."

"Hey! Don't chicken out. No one's seen us."

"No! Let's go back."

"Tell you what. I'll just go nip a piece off the first plant I see, then we'll go. Can't go back empty-handed." He chuckled. He was obviously getting a kick out of the potential danger. Me, I was petrified.

Chad crawled into the brush and was gone for a long minute. Suddenly I heard shouts from the cabin. Chad scrambled out of the brush. "Shit! I tripped on a wire. Let's get the hell outa here."

Chapter Eleven

Not thinking of anything but speed, we made a mad dash for the road. My longer legs put me in front so as I ran, I looked over my shoulder toward the cabin to see if there was any movement there. Suddenly the ground gave way under me and I pitched headlong into a pit. Chad fell in on top of me. We stood up. We were in a chest-high rectangular hole dug in the ground, mounds of dirt piled on either side, a shovel stuck into one pile. The bottom of the hole was soggy and muddy, and made a sucking sound when we pulled our boots out of the mud. We rushed for the end of the pit nearest the road, but the soft earth gave way beneath our boots as we tried to climb out. We fell back, panting.

"I'm taller, so I'll boost you out. Then you pull me," I told Chad.

I lifted Chad and gave him a shove upward to where the smaller boy could get hold of a bush and pull himself out. He turned and reached a hand down to me, and I succeeded in scrambling over the lip of the hole.

Then we ran.

Across the open, moonlit road, up the bank and onto the old logging road we had come down. There was brush along it and we threw ourselves down flat, peeking over the top to see what was happening down below. I had been vaguely aware of the two men shouting to each other. Now I could tell that they had come down the meadow from the cabin, one on either side of the brushy area, searching. As we watched, the man on the far side started back to the cabin, but the one on the road just below us was too close for comfort. We dared not move. Then we heard him call out from a ways up the road, and we got to our hands and knees and scuttled as fast as we could up the old road, heading for better cover and for the horses.

Suddenly, a light brighter than the moon flashed across the meadow.

"Shit. They have a spotlight on their truck," Chad exclaimed.

The spotlight covered the flat, moving systematically, from one side to the other. I thought we should probably get a move on while the men down below were watching the brightly lit area, but the thought came too late. The light swung onto the road and then onto the hillside. It swept across us and moved away. We started crawling on our bellies, but moving even faster than when we had been on hands and knees. When we reached the shelter of some denser brush, we paused. The light swept past again, higher up on the hillside.

"I hope they can't see the horses," I breathed.

"*I* hope the horses don't spook," Chad whispered in response.

The searchers apparently gave up on the hillside and we got to our feet and ran, crouching, to where we had left the horses.

"We'll have to lead them over the hill," Chad whispered. "If your horse sounds like he might snort or whinny, hold your hand over his nostrils." I had a different concern. I remembered how the pinto horse's white rump had shone in the moonlight and was afraid that if the spotlight shone on my horse's large white blaze, it would be clearly visible. I tried to hold him so that his head was turned away from the source of the light. The pickup had moved down the road and was sweeping the area with its spotlight again.

Once we had gotten over the top of the first low ridge, we swung into the saddle and turned down a faint game trail.

"We'll have to keep it to a slow trot until we're out of hearing," Chad murmured. "They can hear horses galloping."

"I hope you know the way."

Chad's laugh was a bit shrill. "Don't worry. We're in the clear now."

When we were sure we had put enough ground between ourselves and the searching men, we hurried our gait, going at either a fast trot or canter, depending on the terrain. The sure-footed ponies seemed to have no trouble seeing, even in the dark patches. We topped the final rise overlooking the valley and our homes. Here we stopped to see if it was safe to go farther.

"They're probably out on the road now, looking for us," Chad said softly.

We saw no light or movement, so keeping to the treed areas we worked our way down toward the road. The last few yards would be over open, moonlit hillside. Chad called a halt while we were in the last shady cover above the open space. Nothing seemed to be moving.

"C'mon." Chad motioned to me.

But just as we were about to step out into the open, I hissed, "Wait! Listen!" We heard the faint hum of a vehicle motor. Hastily, we backed our horses deep into the trees. Below, on the road, a black pickup truck rolled slowly by, its lights off.

"If they go on down the road, we can get to that next patch of shade," I said softly. I saw Chad nod.

We watched the truck ease around a curve in the road and disappear.

"Let's go!"

We dug our heels into the horses' sides, making for the shade of a huge cottonwood alongside the road. I doubted whether it would hide us if the truck came back. And at any time, the men in the truck might shine their bright spotlight into the shady spots along the road. But the truck was out of sight. We looked at each other, doubt still holding us back. Then Chad grinned and said, "Let's go before they come back." He shot out of the shade of the tree onto the road. I was right behind. We were near the T-junction. The truck had gone straight down the road past the place where I lived. We swung onto the road that passed the Monke place, our horses at full gallop. We clattered over the wooden bridge, sounding I thought, loud enough to wake the dead.

We wheeled the horses onto the Monkes' driveway, rode past the house and right into the open barn. As we piled off our sweaty horses, Chad said, "Let's pull the saddles off and turn them out in the corral with the others." We tugged at cinches, flung the saddles along the inner wall, and led our mounts by their bridles out to the corral, letting them loose on the far side of the other half dozen sleepy horses. Back in the barn, Chad grabbed his saddle and hung it by the stirrup on a peg on the wall. I looked for a peg on which to hang my saddle, but before I could find one, the sound of the truck came to us. It was close—very close.

"Get up here by the door!" Chad hissed. I flung the saddle down and ran for the end of the barn nearest the road. We flattened ourselves in the shadow of the front wall of the barn, on one side of the open door.

The truck had stopped at the entrance to the farmyard. The larger of the Monke dogs had greeted us happily when we rode in, but now, with this new arrival, he stalked out toward the road, his hackles up, his lips rolled back showing his teeth. A guttural growl issued from his throat. Plastered against the front wall of the barn, we hardly dared breathe. Then the brilliant spotlight flared up, illuminating the interior of the barn. I looked frantically back at my saddle lying in a heap on the floor. To me it looked as big as a boulder, a dead giveaway. Slowly the light swung over to shine on the corral. The horses, spooked by the sudden, brilliant light, crowded toward the rear of the corral. Would those men see the sweat-stained backs of the horses we had been riding?

The spotlight made another traverse of the corral and barn, and then switched off. But the truck did not move away. We stayed glued to the wall, wondering if the men would get out of the truck and come into the barn. Would they risk the angry dog? I felt Chad inch slowly away. With an effort, I turned my head away from the dangerous mouth of the door to see what Chad was doing. I saw the boy grasp the handle of a pitchfork and ease it down off the wall. Not much of a weapon if the men came in after us.

The motor sound deepened and began to move away. We stayed flattened against the wall until the sound faded into the distance. There was no sound of anyone on foot near the house.

"Okay," Chad spoke softly. "Let's make a dash for the house."

"I've got to hang up my saddle." I hurried back to where I had left it, trying to stay in shadow until I had to move out into the open to grab it. Hastily, I hung it up.

"For Chrissake, hurry."

I scuttled back to our hiding place. We waited a few seconds, then when nothing happened, we made our dash to the house, going in the back door, which like most farm homes had been left unlocked. Without turning on any lights, we scrambled upstairs to a bedroom overlooking the road. Chad moved toward the window, but I grabbed him by the shirttail and pulled him down onto the floor. I had heard the truck approaching again. Now it was quite near. It stopped outside, but there was no spotlight this time. Saving their night vision, I thought, so they could see into the shadows. Would they see the sweaty horses this time?

After what seemed an age, the truck quietly rolled away, its sound overlaid by that of another approaching vehicle, coming down into the valley from the direction of town.

"That's our truck," I exclaimed with relief. "I can tell by the sound."

We tumbled down the stairs, turning on lights as we went. The elder Monkes were getting out of the truck. I dashed out of the house and dived into the back seat. Penny was asleep on the seat, so I sat on the floor.

"What are you doing over here?" Mom asked.

"Oh, we went for a ride in the moonlight then came over here to play computer games," I answered casually. I knew that Chad had handheld games powered by batteries. I'd wanted these myself, but my folks said we couldn't afford to keep getting batteries to run them.

"You were supposed to be in bed." But I could see that Mom was so sleepy, she didn't question my behavior further. Dad stifled a yawn. I was the one who didn't need sleep right now.

At the T-junction, I looked up the road in the direction we had come and saw the black pickup pulled over to the side of the road, in the shade of the large cottonwood. The moon, swinging around to the south, now threw shadow over that portion of the road. Dad didn't even seem to notice the truck, but I ducked down out of sight.

As I got out at our place, the black truck drifted by. I was in plain sight and froze with fear, like an animal caught in the headlights of an oncoming car. But the truck rolled on down the road, and I realized that to be seen getting out of my parents' truck was probably the best thing that could have happened.

Penny had wakened enough to walk to the tent and fall onto her bed, where she promptly fell asleep again. She didn't stir when I crept past her to roll up the side of the tent enough to see the road. Sure enough, the black truck ghosted by again, heading up the valley. I saw it stop at the T-junction for a long minute, then its high beams blazed forth and it rolled away at normal speed. I was still shaking when I climbed into bed, although the danger seemed to be over. After a few minutes, I calmed down and figured that the excitement of the death-defying chase would become something to cherish now that the adventure was over.

Silly me!

Chapter Twelve

I got up at the first sign of daylight and ran over to the Monke ranch. I caught Blaze, saddled him, and rode quietly out of the barn, past the house, and onto the road. The big dog knew me by now and didn't bother me. He gave one soft woof and went back to sleep. By the time I got home and unsaddled Blaze, it was time to milk the cow. Penny stumbled sleepily down the path to the cowshed to feed the animals. She apparently never did know that I had been picked up at the Monkes the night before.

With these long days Penny and I both rebelled at going to bed while it was still light outside. And with the full moon, we were wide awake late into the evening. Mom relented and let us stay up, but insisted that we get up and do our chores at the regular time in the morning. No problem. It was light by then also. After I did the milking the evening after my adventure, Mom thought she ought to send a jug of milk to Grace Herman. Grace used canned milk to cook, but she appreciated the cream from our Jersey cow, a breed noted for the high cream content in the milk. Penny and I set off at about nine o'clock for the Herman house. It was getting dark as we skipped down the road, and the moon was just peeping up over the mountains in the east.

Grace was taking a pan of cinnamon buns out of the oven when we arrived. They smelled delicious. "I baked one pan of them for you folks," she said. "Let them cool a bit. While you wait, would you like some blackberries and cream?"

Would we ever!

"Penny, why don't you go out to the garden and pick some berries. With this moon, it's light enough to see what you're picking, and these bushes don't have thorns. And Derek, would you please split me some kindling?" We always insisted on paying Grace for the food she gave us by doing chores for her.

Penny returned a few minutes later with a big bowl of berries. Grace washed them and removed the stems, adding, "I saved some cream from the last time you brought the milk."

I had never seen milk that wasn't homogenized until we got the cow. I hadn't known that the cream rises to the top. It required a bit of reorganization of my thinking when I first learned that milk does not come from plastic jugs, but only gets there through processing by a dairy. Fresh raw milk was a novelty at first for me, and I was fascinated by how the cream separated itself from the milk when the milk stood around for a while. We also learned something interesting from Grace about raw milk. She told us that we should not store milk in a full bottle in the winter because when it froze it swelled up and needed space. She said that if we let a full bottle with a loose lid freeze overnight, in the morning the lid would be lifted up and sit crookedly on top of a pillar of frozen cream in the morning. I was determined to try this, come winter.

Grace filled two bowls with berries, sprinkled powdered sugar over them, and poured on the rich cream. Boy, was that ever good!

She told us that strawberries and cream were her own children's favourite dessert. "And when Conner Monke and his sister, Darlene, were little, they would come over and I'd feed them strawberries too. I don't think you've met Darlene. She was a very shy girl and she didn't have anyone to play with, so she spent time over here with me. Conner was a nice little boy too, but he spent more of his time with his dad. I never saw much of the younger boy, though."

We went home carrying more berries, as well as the pan of cinnamon rolls.

A couple of days later, I realized that I had not seen Chad since Saturday night. Even if he didn't come over to talk, I would often see him doing the daily check of the cows. But Con had been doing that for the past couple of days. When I next saw Con on the other side of the creek, I hailed him. "Where's Chad? I haven't seen him for a while."

Con called back, "He's gone out to school. The kids here go to high school in Benson's Bridge. He'll be back for Thanksgiving." Benson's Bridge was the next town down the river from Arrow, about sixty miles away.

Chapter Thirteen

It was Wednesday, four days after Chad's and my adventure, when the RCMP showed up. I was helping Dad saw and split firewood, and Mom was in the small herb garden she had planted. She brushed the dirt from her knees and went out to greet the Mountie, a sergeant, who got out of the SUV that the Mounties used for back-country work, and walked toward Mom.

"Mrs. Taylor?"

"Yes. What's the matter?"

"We are looking for a missing person. A young man about six feet tall, slender, with long, blond hair and blue eyes. We are asking everyone who was in town over the weekend if they have seen anyone matching this description. You were in town on Saturday, weren't you?"

"Yes. We went to town for groceries and stayed for the dance. But I don't remember seeing anyone of that description."

"He's a graduate student doing some environmental work. Conner Monke packed him into the mountains a week ago Monday, and brought him out again Friday afternoon. He had left his car at the Monkes' place, and he apparently drove it into town, then disappeared. The car is there, but no one seems to have seen him in town."

"Well, he wasn't at the dance. I'm not sure I'd have noticed him anywhere else."

Dad and I stopped splitting wood and listened to the conversation. We joined Mom and the Mountie.

"Mr. Taylor?"

"No. I don't remember anyone like that."

The Mountie looked at me. I shook my head.

"Derek wasn't with us in town."

"Have you seen any strangers around here?"

Head shakes from all three of us.

"Thanks for your time." The Mountie turned and started to walk back to his vehicle.

I was facing an agony of indecision. Should I mention the hole in the ground? When we were riding home that night from our adventure, Chad had said, "That's a grave, you know!" I had guessed that without him telling me. If I told the Mountie about seeing it, I might have to explain the rest of the incident. I could put it over on Dad, who was easily fooled, but Mom was something else. I thought she could read my mind. Of course, on the other hand, I could puff out my chest and brag about helping the police catch some bad guys. Pride won out.

"Wait!" I shouted. The Mountie turned around, a quizzical look on his face. "I know where there might be a body buried."

"Derek!" Dad admonished. "He doesn't need to listen to any of your stories."

"But..."

"Go back to the tent!"

The Mountie held up his hand. "No. Let's hear what the lad has to say."

"It's like this. Me and another kid went out for a ride in the moonlight Saturday night. We saw a place where he says they grow pot. I don't know whether he knows what he's talking about, but that's what he said. We couldn't see any pot growing, but we did see what looked like a grave."

"Derek!" Dad shouted.

"Go ahead, Derek," the policeman encouraged. "What made you think it was a grave?"

"Well, it was about that size and shape. I saw an empty grave in the cemetery in town once when we went to a funeral, and it looked about the same size. This one wasn't as deep, though."

"This was at night?"

"Yeah, but it was real light. There was a great big moon." That wasn't quite how I remembered it. We'd have seen it, and wouldn't have fallen in, if it had been out in the moonlight, but I wasn't about to admit that part.

"This was an empty grave?"

"Yeah. The shovel was still there."

Mom then threw cold water on my fanciful story. "But if this young man left the area on Friday, even if what you saw was a grave, it couldn't be his."

Undeterred by my parents' objections, the policeman asked, "Do you remember where this place was? Could you find it again?"

"Oh, sure! It's up the canyon where the land sort of levels out and the creek swings way wide out around a sort of brushy meadow. Two guys have a cabin at the upper end. They say it's a mining claim."

"Oh, that place!" Mom exclaimed. "That used to be my favorite fishing hole until those guys built their cabin there. I took my father up there when he came to visit this summer. If you go way out where the creek bends around, it undercuts the bank and makes a deep hole there. You can literally catch your limit in that one spot."

"But you quit going there? Why?"

"When my father and I were out there, one of those guys came down and told us to leave. He was wearing a gun and sort of had his thumbs hooked into the gun belt. We said we had a perfect right to fish there. We weren't interested in gold mining. He just stood there and watched us. It was sort of creepy, so we decided to go on farther down the creek and leave him alone."

"I don't know whether you realize how lucky you are to still be alive," the Mountie said, his expression serious. "Yes, we know that place, and Derek, yes they do grow pot there. Mrs. Taylor, if you had stumbled onto any of their plants, you might be the ones in a grave up there."

"But neither my father nor I would even know what a marijuana plant looked like."

"The man who was watching you wouldn't have known that."

"Oh, my God!" She turned pale.

The Mountie turned to me. "Could you show us exactly where this hole in the ground was?"

"I think so."

"I'll take Derek with me. You folks can come too, if you want." Then seeing Mom's look of distress, he added gently, "It's perfectly safe. Those men have cleared out. I have some men working out there also."

When we came to the brushy area between the road and the creek, I said, "It's near this end, not up by the cabin."

The Mountie drove his SUV off the road into the shade of a large pine tree. Mom pulled up behind us in our pickup. Dad had stayed at home, saying he had work to do and it was probably all a fancy daydream anyway. We all got out.

"Now, can you show me just where this hole was?"

"I think so, especially if I can go up on the hill. That's where we were."

"Okay, go on up."

I walked along the road for a ways, looking for the faint remains of the old logging road, where we had ridden down, and where we had scrambled on our bellies back up the hill. I finally spotted it and pulled myself up the bank, hanging onto brush. It took me a lot longer to get up onto the old logging road than it had done on Saturday night, when we'd had the devil on our tail. I stood up and looked back down toward the brushy area. Unable to spot the place where the grave must have been, I made my way on up the faint road until I reached the clump of brush I could remembered we had hidden behind. I looked down at the vegetation on the flat land, letting my eyes traverse the ground, trying to remember some clear landmark. There was no sign of a grave.

I know it had to be there, because we fell into it, I told myself.

I moved back down, slowly, looking for the tracks Chad and I had made climbing back up onto this old road. A thought struck me. Why didn't the bad guys look for our tracks instead of going up and down the road? It seemed so obvious. We had been so frantically trying to get away that we must have left all sorts of tracks. I couldn't understand why the men who were looking for us had missed what seemed so obvious.

There it was. The grave.

From above, I could make out the oblong of disturbed earth, covered now by brush that was beginning to wilt.

"Hey." I called out. "It's right down there." I pointed. The sergeant moved up the road looking as he went. "A little farther. There. You're right opposite it."

Other policemen had arrived on the scene by that time, and I heard the sergeant giving orders. Two of the new men scrambled down from the road onto the brushy meadow and started moving away from the road at a right angle.

"A little to your left," I called. The men moved on. "You're about there."

A moment later, I saw them halt, move aside a few pieces of brush, and call back to the sergeant, "Yeah, there's a freshly filled in hole here all right. Better send some shovels down."

I sat down on a rock, not willing to go down to where the others stood and lose my grandstand view. The men dug away at the soft earth, sweating in the mid-day sun. Abruptly they stopped and began to brush dirt aside with their hands. One of them straightened up.

"Sarge, you'd better come over here."

The sergeant followed the trail the other men had made, stopping at the edge of the area that had been dug out. The two others continued to move dirt by hand. I could see what looked like a leg, encased in pants with cargo pockets, the foot wearing a hiking boot. The men worked upward along the body. One started to uncover the head. The sergeant turned back to the road and walked back to where Mom was standing. I could hear his voice clearly.

"We owe it to your son. Actually this was not a graduate student gone missing. This man was one of ours, trying to get the low-down on this so-called mining claim. He has been shot in the back of the head."

I saw Mom grab hold of the door handle of the pickup to steady herself.

Suddenly I glimpsed a movement out of the corner of my eye. Turning to look across the canyon to where the steep hillside rose above the opposite side of the creek, I could see a man coming down a trail toward the creek. At least, I thought it was a man. He had a long stride, so I thought he must be tall. I could only see his legs, the upper part of his body being shielded from my sight by tree limbs. He was wearing blue jeans and brown boots. It could be anyone. The man stopped, stood still for a few moments, then turned and hurried back the way he had come. I had a sudden intense fear that the man might have seen me and known that I had been the one to rat to the police. I scrambled down the hillside as fast as I could, and ran to the sergeant.

"Hey, I just saw a man come down the hill over there. When he saw you, he turned around and went back up the hill."

"Do you know who it was?"

"No. I could only see his legs."

"Thanks, son!" The Mountie went to his SUV and could be seen giving orders over the radio. There must be other police around close, I thought, or else he has a really super radio for it to work down in this canyon. The sergeant came back to where Mom and I were standing. He seemed to notice my sudden fear.

"Mrs. Taylor, I think you should take Derek home now. It isn't going to be very pleasant here. We will be by later to get a statement from him. But we are really grateful for his powers of observation. Without his help, we might never have found this grave."

Mom nodded, still unable to speak. The two of us got into our pickup and Mom carefully turned it around and started back down the canyon. When we reached the big meadow, she found a wide spot and pulled over to the side of the road, shutting down the engine. She turned to me. The uncompromising expression on her face was one I knew all too well. It was what I thought of as her dark look, and it boded no good for me.

"Now, young man. I think you have some explaining to do."

Chapter Fourteen

"What were you doing over in that area at that time of night?" There was a no-nonsense tone to Mom's voice. I tried not to squirm, to stay calm and not to give away the dread I felt. I stared straight ahead, out through the windshield, not wanting to look Mom in the eye.

"Chad came over and suggested that we go riding, and since it was such a nice night, I thought it would be fun. We went up on the hillside where we rode in and out of the trees. It looked really weird. Where it was dark, it was really dark. It was like diving into a cave or something. Then when we got adjusted to the dark, we'd come out in the light and it almost blinded us." I thought that by emphasizing that part of our ride, it might throw Mom off the scent. Also, it relaxed me a bit.

"I wouldn't think Chad was the type to be out looking for interesting scenery," Mom pointed out.

I shrugged, trying to look casual.

"Why did you go over to that area where those miners were?"

"We just ended up there."

"You told the policeman that Chad said they grew marijuana there."

"Yeah. When we got over there and saw where we were, he said that."

"You didn't go down there to see?"

I knew that question was coming, and all the time I was rambling on, I was trying to think of an answer. I paused briefly and then it came to me. "We couldn't ride the horses down that steep bank. We had to turn around and go back the way we came. Well not exactly the same way. We came part-way down this side on a different trail so we could ride over to his place." Well, at least that part was true.

Mom seemed to accept that, but she had another issue.

"I really don't like you spending time with Chad. He's a bad influence. I don't like his wanting to use pot, and I don't like his trying to get you to use smokeless tobacco. The next thing he does will probably be to get you to smoke regular cigarettes, which would be bad for your health, and also addictive. You should spend more time with Penny. When Chad is around, you seem to forget about Penny."

"Ah, Mom, he's not that bad. I'm not going to start smoking pot if that's what you're worrying about. And he doesn't smoke because it's dangerous in these dry conditions."

"It's not dry all year round."

Trust Mom to think up a logical answer.

"Besides, who else can I do anything with? If we lived in town, I could meet girls my own age and have dates and go to dances and stuff, and there'd be sports I could get into." That was a sore point with me. Dad wouldn't listen to me if I tried to discuss it with him, but I thought Mom might be on my side. Whenever she was the one who drove into town, she took me with her. I would put on a tight-fitting T-shirt so I could display the muscles I was developing from all the physical work I had to do around the place, and all the chores. I'd strut around town, showing off to any girls I saw. And I'd always go down to the vet clinic and talk to the girl who worked there. "And I'd get to have a computer," I added. "Stuff changes all the time, and you have to keep using them to keep up with what's going on." I'm not so bad at thinking of logical answers myself.

Anyway, the change of subject got Mom off that of my nocturnal adventure. She started the truck and drove on home. I realized later that her questions had been a good warm-up for those the sergeant would ask me when he came back later that afternoon.

Dad wanted to sit in on my interview with the sergeant, whose name was Ross, but I objected. I didn't want my parents around throwing questions at me. I wanted to concentrate on what I was saying to the sergeant. I had to remember what I had told Mom, as well as be prepared for new questions. I didn't want my attention diverted to placating Dad. Ross agreed, as long as either Mom or Dad remained nearby and he could see them.

Another Mountie came with Sergeant Ross and pulled out a notebook to take down what I said. I felt like a criminal being interrogated.

"What's your full name?" I gave it to him; Derek Daniel Taylor.

"How old are you? What's your birthday?"

Those were easy to answer and reminded me of my birthday a month earlier.

"Now, how come you were out riding horses so late at night?"

"It wasn't that late. And I'd seen how pretty the meadow was in the moonlight the night before, so I wanted to see what it was like up in the woods. It was sort of mystic, I guess you'd say. When we could see down into the meadow, it was really beautiful. Actually, it was the other kid's idea to ride up there."

"What is this other boy's name?"

"Chad Monke. He lives at that ranch over there." I waved my arm to indicate the other side of the valley.

"Yes. We know the Monkes. So you rode up into the timber and down the other side of the ridge."

"Yeah."

"Did you come back that way?"

"Yeah."

"Why didn't you ride back by the road? Did the open grave scare you?"

"No. We didn't think of it as a grave," I lied. "It was just a place where someone was digging. I didn't think of it as a grave until you came and told us about that man being missing. Then I wondered if it might have been dug to bury him.

"You didn't see any sign of it being used for that purpose at the time?"

"No. It was just a hole."

"No one was digging in it?"

"No. I think there was a shovel there, though."

"So why did you turn around and go back the way you came? Why didn't you take the road going back?"

"We were going to, but you saw the bank there where that old logging road was cut off when they built the new road. We couldn't ride our horses down that bank, so we turned around and went back over the ridge. Then we took another trail down to the valley."

"Weren't you afraid of getting lost?"

"Oh no. Chad knows all that area really well, and so do the horses. They always want to go back to their barn. Besides it was almost as light as day."

"Was there anyone in the cabin when you got there?"

"Do you mean that one where those miners lived?"

"Yes."

"I could barely see it, but I think there was a light on."

"Did they see you come down that old road?"

"I doubt it. They probably couldn't see us very well. But I didn't really pay that much attention," I lied again. It was becoming easier to lie as time went on. Practice makes perfect, I guess.

"Okay. We'll go talk to young Chad."

"He isn't home. He goes out to high school at Benson's Bridge, so he left on Monday. He'll tell you the same thing I did."

But would he? I wished I could have talked to Chad before either one of us had to be questioned by the police. I was afraid he'd spill the beans and tell all about our harrowing adventure. I later realized that if I'd known the Monkes better, I wouldn't have worried. People of that type can act pretty dumb when asked what they had been doing. Silence was golden, as far as they were concerned.

"Oh well. We'll see him later, if necessary," Ross said. "Thanks for your cooperation, Derek. We owe you. We might never have found that grave without your help."

I heaved a huge sigh of relief, my body instantly relaxing. I hadn't realized how tense I had become, but if the cops noticed that, they showed no sign. Or perhaps they were used to people being tense when they were questioned and then relaxing when it was over.

I hadn't realized what hard work lying could be.

Chapter Fifteen

The Mounties were out at the miners' place for several days. One day, we saw a cube van heading to the area. Later that day they drove out again on their way back to town, we were told, with a load of marijuana plants they had pulled out of the brushy meadow. While they were working in the area, Penny suggested that we ride up there and see what was going on. I was initially wary of going back to the place where I might have been killed if Chad and I hadn't been able to get out of the hole in the ground and up the hillside far enough to hide. But then, my sense of adventure prodded me to go back and observe the area in the light of day.

We trotted up the gravel road. When we reached the bottom end of the brushy meadow, I had a tight feeling in the pit of my stomach. I looked over to the spot where the grave had been. It was now filled in, but was clearly visible from the road. Farther away, I could see the grassy area we had crossed to get to the edge of the brush. The tripwire was still there, now also clearly visible. It was up off the ground enough that a small animal could walk under it. I wondered about deer tripping it, but when I saw how marshy the area was where the brush grew, I realized that deer would not have gone there. They could reach plenty of forage in other areas where they wouldn't have to squish through the soggy ground.

No, the men in the cabin had known that it was a person who had tripped the alarm. At least, when they had come to the gravesite, they would have known. We wouldn't have left tracks on the muddy bottom of the hole, but we would have as we climbed out and ran across the loose dirt at the edge. They would have seen that there were two of us.

We watched the men pulling out pot plants, under the relentless sun. The calendar may have said September, but summer weather was still with us. It might as well have been midsummer, it was so hot. The men stopped and waved to us. What a job! I wouldn't like to be in their boots.

We stopped at the cabin and dismounted.

The other Mountie was outside, sifting through a pile of garbage. Penny went down there to talk to him while I talked to Ross. She peered at the garbage and said, "Ugh." The cop agreed with her.

Sergeant Ross was working inside the cabin, which he seemed to have turned into an office to work from. He came out to talk to me for a few minutes before returning to his work.

"Not scared to come back to the place where a man was buried, eh?" Ross asked, smiling at me. "No qualms about graveyards?"

"Not really. I felt a bit funny about it at first, but I thought if I came during the day, it wouldn't look so much like a graveyard. Actually, if you hadn't come looking for someone who was missing, I probably wouldn't ever have thought of it that way." Yeah, it was getting easier every day to tell little lies.

"What about your sister?"

"Oh, she just thinks this is all really exciting."

"Well, I hope neither of you has any nightmares over it."

"We won't. We're not wimps."

"You couldn't be and live out here."

"Right."

Penny and I said our goodbyes and remounted our horses. As we continued up the road Penny said, "That place is creepy."

"Yeah, it is, isn't it," I agreed. That was the first time I'd seen her show any negative emotion about what had happened. If she only knew what I did, she would have found it more than creepy. Today would be the last time in the two years we lived out on Beaver Creek that either of us ever went past that place.

"Let's go back some other way," Penny suggested.

"Sure. There are lots of trails all over these hills. I've ridden up here a couple of times before."

I led the way up onto the ridge separating this area from the Beaver Valley, looking for the trail that Chad and I had taken. I found a well-used game trail that I thought was it, but it didn't look quite the same in daylight as it had by moonlight. We followed it a ways, but it turned abruptly back to the south, away from the valley. We stopped and surveyed the surrounding country. We were on a different ridge from the one Chad and I had crossed. We listened for any sounds that might have given us an idea whether we were near civilization, but we could hear only the sounds of the forest; a gentle wind sighing in the treetops, birds talking to each other, a chipmunk scurrying up a tree trunk and seeming to scold us for invading his territory. The mid-day sun was in our face, so we were definitely headed south again, while we wanted to go north. Turning around, we headed back along the trail we had come on, but soon it branched out in several directions. We kept to the better-used trails, and tried to work our way down the slope in the direction of the valley. We plunged into deep woods, but before long we came out in a fairly open patch. The trail turned westward, following the contour of the slope. To the north, in the direction we should have been going, we could see no sign of the valley. This did not look familiar to me at all, but I did not want to admit to Penny that I was lost.

Before long this trail, too, branched. The well-travelled trail continued around the contour of the hill, while a fainter one turned to the right, heading downward. I pulled up my horse and surveyed the options. Should we go straight ahead in what might be the wrong direction, or turn down the faint trail that might peter out?

Then I remember Chad's advice; let the horses choose the way. They know where they are and will head back to the barn. I loosened the reins and nudged Blaze with my heels. I would let him pick the trail. At the junction, Blaze turned without hesitation down the faint trail that led in the direction of the valley. After about ten or fifteen minutes, we came out onto a bare outcropping of the ridge. There, spread before us, was a view of the upper part of the meadow. We paused to take in the vista before continuing on. In a short while, we came out of the trees and saw a familiar road right ahead. We joined it a ways above the Herman place and turned toward home. I patted Blaze on the neck and murmured, "Good work."

Grace was out in her garden and waved to us as we passed. Soon after we were home.

"Hey, that was fun," Penny remarked.

"Oh, sure. There are a lot of good places up there to ride," I tried to sound as if I'd planned the route all along.

From then on, however, whenever we wanted to go for a good long ride, I would turn down our small creek to where it joined the larger Jewel Creek, and from there I could choose one of many trails I had become familiar with when riding with Chad.

The police were in and out of the cabin site every day, although I didn't know whether they left anyone watching the site at night. Since so few cars drove through the meadow, we tended to notice them. We especially noticed the police cars as they drove by the Monke ranch, crossed the bridge, and turned left up the road past the Herman place.

One day, I was out riding when I saw Sgt. Ross drive by. No one drives very fast on these gravel roads, so it was easy enough for me to chase his car and catch up with him. He stopped to see what I wanted.

"Hi, Derek. Nice horse you've got there," he said jovially.

"Yeah, I got him from Mr. Monke. He has good horses."

"What's up?"

I leaned over from the back of my horse and talked to him through the open window of his car. "I've been thinking about that guy who was walking down the other side of the canyon when we were out there last Wednesday. Have you found out anything about him?"

"We still don't know who it was. Your description could fit anyone."

"Yeah, I know. I couldn't see anything but his legs. It was someone wearing jeans and brown boots. Not cowboy boots. Work boots."

"But you think it was a man."

"Only because I got the impression from the way he walked that it was someone tall, and that made me think it was a man."

"Can't make much of an ident from that," he said, laughing.

I was a bit disappointed that Sgt. Ross seemed to be dismissing my evidence. I wanted him to take me seriously. I pressed him for more information.

"Is there a trail over there?"

"Not really a trail. There are several places where deer come down to the creek, but no distinct trail."

"The guy looked like he knew where he was going. He wasn't just wandering around."

"He probably was someone who knew the area and was following some indistinct game trail. He might have been a fisherman. You folks probably aren't the only people who know about that good fishing hole."

"I didn't see any fishing rod."

"He might have had it over his shoulder."

"I guess so. But he turned and went away when he saw you."

"There are lots of people who don't really want to be around policemen. Maybe he didn't have a fishing license. But we are still investigating whether anyone else saw someone headed up that way or back out. It probably is nothing of interest to us, but we aren't forgetting about it."

"Okay. Thanks. I was just curious."

Ross drove on, and I watched his car disappear around a bend. I still had a feeling of being let down.

Chapter Sixteen

I didn't see Chad again until Thanksgiving weekend in October. On the first day of the holiday weekend, I saw him doing the daily check on the herd and went out to meet him. When Sgt. Ross first came out there, he must have stopped at the Monke ranch before coming to our place. Chad had already made his hasty departure on Sunday, and I was betting it was to evade being questioned in case our Saturday night adventure came to be known. I'd been worried about that myself, and when Penny and I stopped at the miners' cabin to talk to the Mounties, I asked Sgt. Ross if he could keep my name out of his press releases. Could he just say they found the grave out near the cabin when they were doing their own investigation? I didn't want the man I saw walking down the opposite hillside, and hurrying away when he saw the cops, to know that I had told the cops about the grave. If that man was one of the miners, he would then know that I was the one they were looking for after Chad had tripped the alarm. If that was the case, I didn't want him to come looking for me. The sergeant agreed that my part need not be made public. I didn't want Chad to know either. He might be sore about my ratting to the cops.

But now, Chad was home, at least for the weekend, so I hastily saddled Blaze, rode him across the creek at a shallow spot, and caught up with Chad.

"I missed you. I didn't know you went out to Benson's Bridge to go to school," I said.

"Yeah, had to go to fucking high school. It wasn't so bad when I just went to school in Arrow 'cause I could sneak out and catch a ride part way home if I wanted to," he answered casually. "What ya been doing?"

"Did you know that the cops came out here looking for some guy who was reported missing. They found the grave."

"Yeah, I heard about that. You didn't tell them nothing about what we done, did you?"

"Hell, no. I didn't want to admit I fell into that grave."

"That's good. They found out where I'd gone to and sent a cop over to talk to me. I told him I didn't know nothing about it." He sounded relieved. If he was relieved, I was thanking my lucky stars that Chad had clammed up and not said anything. I didn't want to be associated in any way with the Monkes if they used pot and knew where it was grown. If he'd said anything about wanting to get a sprig off a pot plant, the cops would start questioning him about a lot of other things, things that I would probably get dragged into.

Chad was back the next weekend, and again I saw him riding through the cattle. He forded the creek and rode over.

"Hi," I called out. "I didn't think you'd be back again until school was out for Christmas."

"I don't go to school no more."

"Oh. Why?"

"I got kicked out," he said gleefully.

I didn't answer. I figured he'd tell me anyway. After a few minutes of idle chatter, Chad finally asked me, "Hey Derek. Have you had a girl yet?"

I glanced at him, frowning. He was chuckling and I knew he was probably bursting to tell me something juicy. I asked, "What do you mean?"

"You know. Have you ever fucked a girl?"

"Of course not."

"Well, you should try it. I done it. That's how I got kicked out of school. Me and this girl went out into the bushes behind the school one night when there was a school party on. We'd just got started when this big kid came out there with his girl and chased us out. Then he came back and told everyone. He was laughing at us. Well, the principal heard about it and he kicked me and the girl out of school for the rest of the year. He didn't kick that big guy or his girl out, though, and everyone knew they were doing it, too."

"That doesn't seem fair."

"What the hell. I don't care. I'm happy I don't hafta go to school no more. And I got the better of the principal anyways. Me and the girl went to her house while her dad was off at work and her mom was out shopping and done it there."

As I listened to his bragging, I wondered what Mom would have thought about this conversation if she had heard it.

But Chad had brought up a problem that had become a bone of contention with me. I was maturing physically, and wanted to be where I could meet girls and have dates with them. I would be starting high school a year from now, and I was trying to figure out how I could get my folks to let me go away to school like the other kids who lived out in the bush did.

Of course, if my parents ever heard Chad talking like this, I knew I'd never be allowed to do so, at least not to the high school in Benson's Bridge, the town down the river from Arrow.

A few days later, Chad came over again. He told me in a bitterly dejected voice, "My dad went down to the high school and gave them hell for kicking me out, so they said I could come back. Damn! I'm mad at my dad. I thought I had it made."

The next day, he was gone again.

Chapter Seventeen

Bill Herman told us he would get hold of a horse logger who would bring his team over and help us haul in a few trees to cut up into firewood. One day, an elderly man arrived at our tent.

"I'm Woody," he said.

"Oh. You're the horse logger, aren't you?"

"Yep."

"Can you skid some trees for us for firewood?"

"Yep."

"When can you come?"

"Tomorrow."

A man of few words, obviously.

We needed to scout out some suitable trees to use for this purpose. We looked for dead trees, either fallen or standing, found three windfalls, and got them ready to be skidded out to where we could saw them into stove wood lengths.

Bill arrived with a chain saw, to Dad's dismay. Dad considered chain saws to be noisy, awkward modern objects, and he wanted only to use a crosscut saw. But Dad respected Bill, and didn't want to offend him, so he kept his mouth shut. Bill cut each windfall from its roots. The roots then settled back into the hole it had been pulled out of by the weight of the falling tree. Dad and I cut off the branches and tops in preparation for the team to pull it out.

The next day Woody returned with a matched pair of Belgian horses, big fellas with hairy legs and long manes, curried until their coats shone, and their manes and tails combed. They were grey in colour, and matched their grey-haired owner. Penny fell in love with the horses. They seemed to love her in return, but that may have been because of the pocketful of carrots she brought with her. Woody lifted her onto one of the horses and let her ride into the woods.

Woody wrapped a large chain around the butt of a log, backed the horses into position, and hooked them up. Before he gave the horses the signal to start pulling, he looked over to where Penny and I were watching and yelled, "Keep back." We moved farther back into the woods. He slapped the reins onto the horses' rumps and whistled to them. They dug in their front hooves, lowered their heads, and leaned into their collars. The log gradually began to move. When it was in motion, the horses settled into the gait that would keep it going. The top of the tree swung around toward us as the team rounded a corner. We could see why Woody yelled at us, as the top of the tree whipped viciously around in our direction. We followed along behind and watched Woody nimbly hop from one side of the log to the other to avoid it rolling on his legs. He was amazingly spry for an old man. The team stopped where we planned to saw up the logs and Woody unfastened the chain, pulled on the left hand rein and clucked to the horses. They walked easily away.

"How'd they know they weren't still supposed to pull?" Penny asked.

"Turn 'em." Woody said.

When he had skidded out three logs for us, Woody collected his pay and watered his horses.

Mom remarked, "You must really love those horses, the way you treat them. They look great."

"Can't live without 'em." For Woody, that was a long sentence.

He refused an invitation to lunch, and left. He'd said only about ten words all day.

After lunch, Dad and I took the crosscut saw he had bought at the yard sale in Arrow and started to cut the logs into firewood lengths. Man, it was hard work! We started at the large end of one of the logs. We hadn't even got half way through the first cut when we had to stop. I was drenched with sweat and my shoulders were screaming with pain. Bill stopped by, and seeing us, came over to help. He took my end of the saw and after one pass through the log he stopped.

"Jesus Christ! This saw's dull. Here, lemme show you guys how to sharpen it."

Dad fetched him a vice and attached it to the wooden picnic table. Bill went to his truck and came back with files and a device for checking that the teeth were level with each other. It was a slow job, done meticulously. When he finally finished he took me with him and said, "Let's start at the small end. No use doing the hardest job first. Leave that till you're more experienced." We started the cut and the saw sang through the wood, sawdust flying in both directions. Our first block of wood fell off in no time. "There. You gotta have your tools in good shape, or you'll end up doing a lot more work than you need to." Just one of the many kinds of sound advice Bill Herman gave us. We would never have survived without him, I don't think.

For the next few days, Dad and I were busy splitting and stacking enough wood to last, we hoped, until spring. We went to work right after breakfast, stopped at mid-day for a sandwich, and worked until it started to get dark. I've never worked so hard in my life. I ate like there would never be any food again and I gained weight, but it was all muscle.

Chapter Eighteen

Winter came early to the valley. Usually, the weather cools off slowly for several weeks before getting really cold. But it had been warm throughout most of October, and when an arctic cold front roared through late in the month, we weren't ready for it.

We returned on a winter day to our tent, after we had all gone to town. We stepped inside to find that it was almost as cold as outside. Even the water in the bucket, with a dipper hanging beside it, was frozen over.

The first thing we thought about was to get a fire going. Penny and I were sent out to get more wood and fill up the wood box so there would be enough to last the night. Mom and Dad took off their gloves, left their coats on, and set about starting a fire. This consisted of putting crumpled newspaper in the firebox, placing kindling on top of it, then adding small pieces of firewood. Once the fire started burning, larger chunks of wood were added. The wood-burning kitchen stove provided heat for the tent as well as being our stove for cooking, so once the fire started putting out heat, we opened the oven door, placed a stick of stove wood on it, and took turns propping our feet, still in their wool stockings, on the wood in order to warm our feet. Once the fire was going well, Mom put on a pot of coffee and started fixing dinner.

"Darn it," she said. "I wanted to get the ashes cleaned out of the stove while it was cold. It won't burn well unless we do. I'll shake them down into the collection box tonight, and you kids can clean it tomorrow."

I groaned. Cleaning out the ashes is a dirty job, consisting of raking them into a bucket or pan and carrying them outdoors, then sweeping up any that had fallen on the floor. This was one of the jobs that fell to us kids.

The next morning, the ashes were still hot when I raked them out, and Mowser was lying under the stove. A hot coal landed on his back, and he let out a blood-curdling yowl. Dad was just coming in the door. Mowser saw the opening, dashed out the door, and beat it for the safety of the hay shed. Penny cried out, "Poor Mowser." Then, ever practical, she added, "Oh, no! He might set the hay on fire if any of his hair is burning."

"I don't think so," I replied. "I didn't see any fire or smoke." But Penny hastily put on her coat and went looking for Mowser anyway. Coaxing him out of the hay, she examined him carefully, but found only a bit of singed fur. It was several days before he agreed to come back into the tent, though Penny called, trying to coax him to come with her, every time she went to the barn to feed the horses and the cow. He had a nice cozy nook in among the bales of hay, and seemed quite comfortable there.

Penny's part of the ash cleaning job was to get rid of the ashes. After she came back from inspecting Mowser for burns, she took the pan of ashes and spread them on the path to the barn. A recent rain left the path wet, and it then froze into a sheet of ice when the cold weather hit.

For the next few days, we stayed in the tent, keeping the wood box stocked and the fire roaring in the stove. We only went outside to do our chores, and to carry more wood into the house. I was amazed at the amount of wood, which I had so laboriously chopped during the summer, that stove could burn up in the course of a single day. We didn't use the stove much during the summer because one of the problems with using a wood stove is that if you want to cook, you also have to heat your home, even if it is the hottest day of the summer. In the fall, we often let the fire go out during the day, and only used it to cook meals and heat the tent in the mornings and evenings.

Simple life, ha! In our house in Idaho, when it got cold, all we had to do was turn up the thermostat.

Chapter Nineteen

Fallen trees came into our lives again on the last week in November.

On a cold, dreary night the wind came up, howling through the treetops and sending every loose object flying. I hurried as fast as I could down the icy path to the barn for the livestock, but found them unconcernedly munching on their hay. They could get out into the open area of the pasture if they had to. Mowser stuck his head out from between bales of hay, greeted me with a brief meow and returned to his cozy nook. The animals did not seem bothered at all by the rising wind, but we humans were spooked by the noise and the realization of the danger we would be in, should a tree fall on our tent. No one went to bed that night. We all sat up and listened to the wind.

We had planned to build the house out in the open, away from any trees that might fall. We had erected the tent in another spot so that work on the house could proceed without the tent being in the way. Living in a tent was meant to be a short-lived proposition, but our house wouldn't be built for nearly a year. It was now unnerving to see the trees to the windward of us swaying and bending in the wind.

"They have been growing there for years," Dad blustered. "They haven't fallen yet, and I'm sure this isn't the first windstorm that's hit them." We kids and Mom tried to believe that he was right.

I could hear trees falling in the timbered area above the road; first a drawn-out cracking sound followed by a heavy thud as the tree hit the ground. Penny started to count them, but lost track at some point. It must have been about eleven o'clock when we heard the cracking sound of tree limbs breaking off as a falling tree rubbed against other trees, a lot closer than any we had heard so far. The sound came from the group of trees closest to us, directly west of our tent. We all froze, as if we were in some scene frozen in time. We heard the sound of tree roots ripping out of the ground. Mom gasped.

Suddenly Dad shoved back his chair and headed for the door He hesitated, however, before he reached it. Mom snaked out her hand, pulled the propane lantern toward her, and turned it off. At least, if the tree fell on the tent, it wouldn't set the whole place on fire. With the tent plunged into darkness, we waited. It seemed like ages, but was really only seconds, before the large tree thudded to the ground almost literally in our laps. The ground shook, rattling the dishes in the cupboard.

Mom relit the lamp and we could see a branch of the tree pushing through the mangled door, right where Dad would have been had he reached it. The trunk of the tree was lying across in front of the tent, missing it by no more than two or three feet.

"We've got to get out of here," Dad said. "Get your coats on and let's run to the truck." We bundled ourselves into our warm clothes, broke off enough branches to be able to get out the door and climbed over others until we rounded the corner of the tent and could reach open ground. Mom was carrying the lantern, which she had relighted. She turned it off again as soon as we could make out a clear path to the truck, parked on the side of the road.

"Where to?" Dad asked. "Somewhere in the open."

"The Hermans," Mom replied calmly.

"Oh. Of course." Dad sounded as if he hadn't even thought of going to someone else's home. The Hermans' house was in the open, not threatened by falling trees. So was the Monkes'.

There were other pickup trucks parked in the Hermans' yard. I recognized the old heap driven by Woody Woodruff, the elderly horse logger who had dragged the trees in for us to saw up into firewood. The other turned out to belong to Steve Carlssen, a young man who had moved from Arrow to a place near the top of the divide between here and town.

Grace met us at the door and hugged each one of us. "We were so worried about you. You're the last ones to get here. Everyone else is here already." She bustled around getting coffee for the adults and cocoa for Penny and me, while Bill took our coats and hung them up.

Steve came over to meet us. "Hi. I'm Steve. I've met Phil, but not the rest of you. Glad to know you." He was a tall, broad-shouldered young man with curly blond hair. I figured he must have had all the girls in Arrow chasing him, he was that good-looking.

So this was the man who had aroused Mom's anger earlier in the fall. Well, actually she wasn't mad at Steve himself, only at Dad. Dad, on his trips into town, had stopped by on several occasions to help Steve build the house where Steve would bring his new bride. I could remember the storm clouds that rolled across Mom's face when Dad had told her why it had taken him so long to get back from town and she acidly remarked, "You can spend hours of your time helping that guy build his house, but every time I ask you when you're going to start on ours, you have some excuse for not doing so." The atmosphere around our place had been frosty for a week afterward.

It would be hard to stay angry with Steve. He was a pleasant, always smiling young man. Even Mom was on friendly terms with him within minutes of meeting him.

Knowing that both Steve and Woody lived along the road to town, and they had passed the Monkes' ranch to get here, Mom asked them why they hadn't stopped there.

"Don't like Monke," was Woody's gruff answer.

"I don't care much for him either," Steve said. "Abe Monke will cheat you, any time he can. And that older boy, Con, is like him. Erma is all right. I kinda feel sorry for her, living out here with those men. Her daughter ran away and got married to get out from under her dad's thumb. And that younger boy, Chad, he's a right little shit." He looked suddenly embarrassed and said to Mom, "Oops! Sorry."

"You don't need to apologize. I've heard language like that before."

Grace brought food to us, and Bill supplied beer to the men. The party atmosphere lasted far into the night. Eventually, though, Steve and Woody rolled up in blankets and slept on the living room floor, leaving the couch for me. Penny slept with Mom and Dad in the second bedroom.

In the morning, I was awakened by the smell of bacon frying. Grace put a big plate of bacon, a platter of eggs, and a huge mound of pancakes on the table, and everyone dug in. Coffee cups seemed to refill automatically.

Steve and Woody left right after breakfast, anxious to see whether their cabins were still standing. We heard later that all was well at their homes.

Before they left, Penny, who had taken a liking to Woody and sat beside him at breakfast, asked him, "What about your horses? You must be worried about them."

"Barn's okay," he reassured her.

Steve interpreted, "Woody's barn is in an open space. It's his house that's up in the trees."

"Oh, good. I'm glad they're okay," Penny replied, relief in her voice.

Even Penny and I had coffee that morning, on the premise that we needed hot food and drink in our stomachs as we headed out again into the cold. The wind had subsided, but the temperature had dropped to minus twenty degrees Celsius. Penny promptly translated that to the Fahrenheit scale, which we were more used to, having moved here from the States, and told us it was only four degrees below zero. Somehow that didn't sound quite as cold as minus twenty.

When we arrived at our tent, Dad got an axe from the woodshed and started chopping limbs off the fallen tree, with Mom piling them over near the standing trees.

Penny and I left for the livestock shed, where the cow was mooing in distress because of her distended udder and the horses were whinnying for their morning feed. We usually milked the cow and fed the animals when we first got up, so we were really late today. I took the milk bucket from where it hung under the shed roof and started to work. I found that I couldn't milk with my gloves on, but as soon as I removed them, my hands began to freeze. They got too cold for me to continue before I got the cow's udder completely empty.

"Sorry, girl," I told her. "I'll do a better job tonight."

It was so cold that in the short walk back to the tent, a few crystals of ice were already forming on the surface of the milk.

Dad and Mom had a path cleared to the battered door of the tent. Inside, it was as cold as outside. Mom hastily built a fire in the stove and picked up the coffee pot to fill it.

The water bucket was frozen over and Dad had to come from his task of repairing the door to break the ice with his hammer. It took a long time for the coffee to perk.

Eventually the stove was putting out heat, the tent door was crudely repaired, and we could take turns sitting in front of the open oven with our stocking feet propped up on a piece of wood on the oven door. Mowser came in and found a warm spot under the stove. We never took our coats off all day.

Chapter Twenty

On Christmas Day, Grace served us a turkey dinner with all the trimmings. Steve and Woody were there, too. It had snowed heavily the day before and Steve did not want to risk driving to Caribou where his new wife was staying with her mother until their baby was born. Steve worked at the sawmill in Arrow, and often drove to Caribou on weekends to visit. It would be spring before he could bring his wife and child home.

For the rest of the winter we hunkered down to survive the cold and the snow, discovering that four people confined to a sixteen by twenty foot tent makes for a lot more togetherness than we had imagined. The only thing Penny and I had to relieve the monotony was our schoolwork. But we got through our lessons much more quickly than we would have in a public school. We did a lot of reading.

I often thought that this simple life might be the death of us yet.

We brought a battery powered radio with us when we moved to Beaver Creek, but we used it sparingly to save the battery in case we ever needed it to hear vital broadcasts in case of an emergency. We listened regularly to morning and evening news broadcasts, but we didn't use it for anything else. We were unable to recieve most radio stations since they were predominantly FM, and FM was another of those line-of-sight things that we couldn't receive here in the valley. We could get one AM station that broadcast from southern Alberta, and that was where we kept up to date on the news.

The music it broadcast didn't appeal to Mom and Dad anyway, though we kids would have listened to it.

We didn't hear any mention on the radio of the Beaver Creek murder, as it was called, all winter, but then, it was not an Alberta crime, so the station was probably not interested in it. Occasionally, there was an article in the Caribou paper about the murder, but it didn't tell us much. The reports were mainly repetition of the earlier news.

The cops were still looking for those guys who were mascarading as miners, thinking one of them was probably the guy who murdered the undercover cop. I know that the police work very hard at finding the perpetrator if the victim is a cop, so I supposed that they were beavering away, but we did not hear anything about their search.

Penny and I did find another source of recreation on a late winter day when it was half raining, half snowing. There was a pile of lumber left over from building the animal and hay sheds. I think it was Penny's idea to build a raft and float down the creek, but I agreed enthusiastically.

I got hammer and nails and went to work. We carried the raft down to the bank of the creek and launched it, carefully climbing aboard while one end was still on the bank. We floated down one of the large pools, being careful to remain sitting in the centre of the raft. All went well until we reached the first place where the creek became both shallow and narrow, causing the speed of the water flow to increase. Where the water was forced into the narrower channel, it became higher on the sides, and we could feel the raft tipping to the left. Penny was sitting in front of me and I was holding onto her. We leaned over to the right, but that caused us to slide to the left. Penny let out a whoop as the left side of the raft dipped underwater, flipping us instantly into the cold water of the creek.

We both surfaced, laughing, as we watched our raft, now upside down, sail on down the stream without us. We waded to shore.

"I wonder how far it will go," I said, spluttering while I tried, not very successfully, to dry my face with the sleeve of my coat.

"Maybe it will go all the way to the ocean," Penny said.

"I doubt it. It'll hang up somewhere and we can go get it later."

We walked home, our clothes soaked through. Our coats were supposed to be waterproof on the outside, but they weren't on the inside and had filled up with water when we slid into the creek. We didn't get cold walking home, though. Our bodies warmed the water next to our skin and during the short walk back to the tent, we felt quite cozy.

We thought it had been great fun, but Mom's view of our escapade was much different. For days, the clouds were nearly down to the ground, and the humidity must have been at least ninety-nine percent. As a result, clothes did not dry, even when hung on a rack near the fire for days. We were pretty much confined to the tent anyway. With no water repellent coats to wear, there was no choice but to stay indoors except to do routine chores, like milking the cow, feeding the livestock, and carrying wood to fill the wood box. We were all getting a little stir-crazy anyway, and it didn't help Mom's mood when Penny and I relived our experience amid gales of laughter.

Penny and I went down the creek looking for the raft on the first day the weather permitted. We found it impaled on Stone's fence, but we couldn't retrieve it, because the weather had turned cold and the raft was frozen to the wires of the fence. We sort of conveniently forgot about it after that until months later when Old Stoneface turned up at our tent, purple in the face with anger, and accused us of, well, I'm not sure what. Several days after Stone returned for the summer, he stormed over to our place and griped angrily that our raft had ended up caught in his fence where the fence extended into the creek.

"Why don't you keep an eye on what your brats are doing," he yelled at my parents.

It made me mad that he had just assumed that we were the culprits. But Dad, knowing that we were indeed guilty, tried to placate him and said he would go down to Stone's place to retrieve the raft.

"Just don't damage my fence while you do it."

When Dad left on his errand, Mom laid into us. We had to listen to her recite a litany of our sins as she let off steam. But she had a few choice words to say about Old Stoneface as well.

Chapter Twenty-One

In late March, the weather broke. The sun came out, the temperature rose, and the trickle of water in the gullies became raging streams carrying the snowmelt down from the higher mountains. Grass began to grow, we saw a doe with a spindly fawn walking along beside her, and there were more white-faced calves beside the Monke cows every day. Our horses ran and bucked their way around the pasture. Life was returning to the valley.

Spring also meant spring-cleaning. For us, that involved cleaning the soot out of the stovepipe. This is a tedious and dirty job. Guess who got to do it.

Since we couldn't put a stovepipe through the tent roof, when Dad and Bill built the framework for the tent, they left an open spot in the wooden framework at a point where the stove would be installed. The stovepipe was led out through this opening before turning upward. Sheet metal was used to surround the stovepipe, so that it didn't touch the wood.

To clean the stovepipe, the guy wires attached to the roof were disconnected, and the pipe dismantled piece by piece. The places where soot collected the most were the right angle bends, one where the pipe attached to the stove, one outside the tent where the pipe turned upward, and in the section of pipe that held the damper.

If there had been running water under pressure, the job would have been much easier. But all the water had to be carried from the spring in buckets, by me, so I didn't want to waste any of it. I wore old jeans and T-shirt to do the job, and both were filthy by the time I was done. I also had smears of soot on my face and even in my hair.

Penny sat by and watched me work. She seemed to think it really amusing. I figured that she was rejoicing that she didn't have to do the work. Once, when I muttered a word that I was not supposed to use, she shook a finger at me and said, "Naughty, naughty," then added, "But I won't tell on you."

"Oh, shut up," I snarled. "If you think it's so funny, come over here and help me do it."

She continued to heckle me, and when I finished the job, I went over to her and rubbed my filthy hands on her blonde hair before she could get away. Revenge always feels good.

There seemed to be a never-ending supply of chores that needed to be done. Every season of the year brought on a different set of them. To think that when we lived in town, I used to grumble about having to roll the garbage bin out to the street.

You will hear people say that having children do chores is a way of teaching them responsibility. That's a bunch of bunk. The reason the kids get stuck with splitting wood, carrying water, and shovelling manure, (and cleaning stovepipes), is that adults hate those chores as much as kids do, but being bigger and smarter, they are able to pass the buck.

One Saturday, Steve Carlssen arrived with a cement mixer in the back of his truck and helped Dad build the foundation of our new house. The next weekend, he was back with three pickup loads of fellow sawmill workers from Arrow, and a truckload of lumber. In one day, they built the floor, raised the walls, and put on the roof. In went the windows and doors. On Sunday a certified electrician arrived with them. He wired the house for one overhead light and one wall outlet for each room and connected them to the gasoline-powered generator that Mom had demanded. She had seen how much better the light was in the Herman and Monke houses. They used larger generators, ones that would even run fridges. Ours was a smaller one and we had to be careful not to plug in more than one appliance at a time. It wouldn't run a fridge, much less a stove, nor could we use a computer. Laptop computers weren't as common then, and were too expensive, according to Dad. He vetoed our trying them. Dad kept saying that he would put solar panels on our roof so we would have a better form of electricity, but I knew Mom wasn't holding her breath until it was done, and neither were Penny and I. Dad was too easily distracted, and it might be years before he ever got around to doing it.

We now had a real house to live in. We'd eventually have running water, but our spring, where the water came from, provided only enough water for one faucet in the kitchen. We would have to sink a well before we could have a bathroom with a toilet, and we still had to use the stove to heat water. But our level of comfort vastly improved.

On the ground floor were a living room, a bedroom for Mom and Dad, a large kitchen, and a room set aside for the future bathroom, but which was now being used as a pantry. The loft overhead, reached by a ladder, was divided midway into bedrooms for Penny and me. The walls were insulated, and fibreglass insulation was placed on the underside of the roof. Due to a mistake in measuring, the sheet-rock fell short of covering the insulation for the whole extent of the roof. Penny's room, at the front of the house, got the full treatment, but at my end, several thicknesses of newspaper tacked over it held the insulation in place. Thank heavens for those nice fat issues of the Saturday *Globe and Mail* that Old Stoneface used to drop by for us during the previous summer. We didn't have quite enough newspaper, especially since we also used it to start the fire in the kitchen stove. But sure enough, Old Stoneface brought us some more when he returned for this summer. We also bought the skimpy local paper, and the Caribou paper, whenever we went into town. I used to lie awake on my bed and read the news upside down.

During a break for lunch at the house-raising, Steve came over to the tent where Mom, with Grace Herman's help, was doling out sandwiches to the hungry crew, including me. "Hey, I heard that Abe Monke gave that little kid a whipping," he told us. "He wouldn't have been able to do it to Con, because Con was almost as big as his dad at that age, but Chad's a little runt."

"What did the boy do?" Dad asked.

"He got hold of Con's supply of joints and had been smoking them for days while Con was away."

"So his dad wasn't happy about his son smoking pot?"

"It wasn't that. It was because the stuff was for sale, and Chad was smoking up the profits." Steve seemed to find that funny.

"Do you mean that Monke is a drug dealer?"

"Him and Con both. Some of the guys I work with buy from Con. But don't worry. I don't use it, and I told them not to smoke the stuff when they come out here." That seemed considerate of him. I was wondering where Chad went to smoke, considering his lecture to me about not dropping matches or cigarette butts on the ground or in the barn. My question was answered when I watched a couple of the sawmill workers grabbing a quick smoke (tobacco, not pot) before getting back to work. They rolled up the bottom of one leg of their Levis and used that for an ashtray. Heavy denim does not burn easily.

That night, I heard Mom and Dad talking. Mom said, "I don't think we should let Derek hang around with that Monke boy when he comes back home when school is out this summer."

"We can't really tell him not to," Dad replied. "There aren't any other kids Derek's age around here."

"If we lived in town, he'd have other boys to be friends with."

"They'd probably smoke pot, too, and heaven knows what other drugs they'd use. I don't think that Monke kid is any danger to Derek."

"If we were in town, there would be a lot more boys who don't use drugs than there would be ones who did, and we could make sure he associated with the right kids."

"Well, we're not moving back to town, and that's that!"

Mom never answered back when Dad laid down the law about where we would continue to live. But Dad was right. I'd never let Chad Monke persuade me to smoke pot, I assured myself.

Chapter Twenty-Two

Life settled down into a routine as summer arrived in the valley. The days started to get light before four o'clock in the morning. By mid-morning, it began to get hot, the sun shining relentlessly out of a clear deep blue sky. It remained very warm well into the night, but then the temperature dropped continuously through the rest of the night, making it quite chilly by early morning. Dew would form on the meadow, sometimes creating a knee-deep layer of mist. The days were so long, it was hard to get sleepy enough to go to bed until well into the night. Because of the clear air, the stars were visible by the millions on moonless nights, with the Milky Way forming a brilliant river across the sky.

Daily life became pretty routine. I began to wish more and more that I lived in town, where I could play baseball, swim in a real pool, picnic in the evening on a beach or in a park, and ride a bike. I hadn't ridden a bike in over a year. We sold our bikes before moving, but we were outgrowing them anyway, with Penny eyeing my bike for herself when I got a bigger one. I wanted a bright red racing bike so I could enter the bike races that were becoming popular.

My daydreams always included other kids. Everyone else got summer off from school, but I never got time off from my isolation out here. Or from the chores. I don't know how Penny felt about it, but I yearned for contact with other kids my age. My parents, however, showed no inclination to give up on this isolated life.

Even with the good weather allowing us to spend a lot of time outdoors, we were all suffering from cabin fever, so on a day in late June, we decided to make a family trip to Arrow. Arrow is a very small town, but after a winter on Beaver Creek, it seemed like the height of civilization. We picked up the mail, Dad picked up and sent his faxes, and we had lunch in the café. The last store we went to before leaving Arrow for home was the hardware store, which was actually more of a general store. It seemed to sell everything except groceries. Dad needed some tools, and things like nails and screws. Mom saw a poster in the window advertising a fly-fishing club that was offering lessons to beginning anglers. Interested, she asked the clerk, who was the store's owner, about the club. He let out a snort of derision

"That's for a bunch of rich guys who want to pretend to be outdoorsmen and buy a bunch of fancy rods and reels, and things to test the water for this and that, and want to try out the latest fly they've read about. All you need to catch fish in these creeks is a hook and some earthworms."

"Yeah," I remarked. "That's all I use and I catch my limit every time. There are lots of worms in the manure pile."

"There. You see. Forget about that fancy stuff."

Mom didn't seem too pleased about being reminded of one of the less savoury aspects of rural life, so I thought I'd help her out. "I'll dig the worms for you, Mom, when you want to go fishing."

"Thanks, Derek." Her tone of voice made me think she really didn't cherish the gift of having worms dug for her out of a manure pile.

Later in the summer, a van with the name of the fly-fishing club on it passed our place on its way down into the canyon where Beaver Creek emptied into the larger Jewel Creek. Bill was at our place and saw them pass. He told us, "They bring newcomers out here to Jewel Creek to teach them how to fly fish. Dunno if they ever catch anything."

That gave me an idea.

I caught my horse and saddled him. I left his rope halter on underneath the bridle and looped the lead rope around his neck. I wore old cut-off jeans and old scuffed tennis shoes instead of my cowboy boots. I dug some worms and put them in a flat box I could stuff into my shirt pocket, and added a plastic envelope with several hooks and a length of fishing line. I didn't take a fishing rod, but slipped the sheath of a good hunting knife onto my belt. Thus provisioned, I headed for Jewel Creek.

The gravel road looped up around the open area bordering the creek to a spot where the rocky banks provided a solid foundation for supporting the bridge. The stream ran in shallow ripples alongside the road. Spread along this open area were five fishermen practicing their casts. They were spaced far enough apart, two on the far side, three on the near, so that they wouldn't catch each other's lines. A sixth was helping one man with his gear. I turned downstream a short distance to where a huge boulder had at some time in the past rolled into the creek, blocking it. The water had scoured out a deep pool upstream from the rock, letting a small trickle around it on the far side. There was a pebble beach above the pool. Summer days in the west can be very hot, and fish would seek the cool shade deep in the water beneath the edge of the rock.

I tied Blaze to a small tree where there was both shade and grass. With my knife, I cut a long, straight stem from a bush, removed all the small limbs except one at the end to keep my line from sliding off. I put a hook with a small silver spinner, to catch the fish's attention, on the other end of the line, baited it with a worm, and walked down to the tiny beach.

"Hey, kid, you can't fish here. This is our territory." It was the sixth man of the fishing group.

"This is a public stream. Anyone can fish here," I replied.

"We have this area reserved."

"Oh. From who?" I shudder at what the teacher who graded my English lessons would say had she heard me.

"Never you mind. Just beat it."

His threat didn't disturb me; not like the fake miner's threatening stance that forced Mom and Grandpa to leave the fishing hole beside their grow-op. Instead I turned my back on the man, went to the bank of the stream and tossed the baited hook into the water. The current carried the hook toward the rock, and down deep into the water. The sudden jerk on the line nearly pulled my makeshift rod right out of my hand. I grabbed for it and started pulling in the fish, a huge trout. I pulled it onto the pebble beach, grabbed it by the gill, conked it over the head with a rock, and laid it on the grass beside the beach. I glanced toward the man who had been berating me. He was standing there, hands on hips, a scowl like a thundercloud on his face. I put another worm on my hook and headed back to the creek. I knew he couldn't really do anything about me fishing there. The next time I turned to look for him, he was walking back to his group.

I caught my limit, six trout, within fifteen or twenty minutes. Three of them were whoppers. I cut another branch, removed smaller branches, leaving one small one at the lower end, and slipped my fish onto it, leaving enough room at the upper end to hold onto. By this time, all six of the fishermen were standing a few yards away, staring in awe at the kid who had caught his limit. I hadn't seen any of them catch a single fish.

Riding back home, I had to pass Old Stoneface's cabin. He had returned for the summer and was out in his yard. I held my fish where he could see them, sort of taunting him, and the scowl on his face was even uglier than that of the boss of the fishing club.

Chapter Twenty-Three

Old Stoneface returned to his cabin on the last Saturday in June, when the school year ended. We saw him drive by in his white SUV. A couple of hours later, he walked up to our place, bringing with him a copy of the weekend edition of the *Globe and Mail*, a national newspaper. We always enjoyed reading it when he brought us one. The stores in Arrow didn't carry it. Its articles always had more detail than those of any local paper we could get. Mom and Dad would read it from front to back, and I liked to read it, too. Dad invariably complained about the news always being the same, and insisting that newspapers weren't worth reading, listing the subjects that always seemed to be in the papers Stone brought us. But he would go through them thoroughly, nonetheless.

Once everyone had read the paper, I would tack it, two pages thick, over the insulation on the underside of the roof over my bedroom. We used masking tape to hold the rectangles of insulation in place, but it sometimes gave way. One night, I was awakened by a piece of insulation falling onto my face. I struggled to get whatever it was that was trying to smother me off my face, only to find that I had been attacked by a pink panther.

With this latest paper Stoneface brought, I now had about two thirds of my ceiling covered, so I guess the man was useful for something.

Every time I rode by Stoneface's cabin, I tried to see whether there was any way to get into his workshop, but when he was working there, he shut the door, and I wondered if he locked it from the inside. If he happened to be in his yard when I rode by, he would stand and glare at me until I moved out of range. My curiosity was killing me. More and more, I was dying to get into that workshop, but I couldn't see any way of doing so.

Stone would occasionally walk up to our place to talk to Dad. They were both dedicated environmentalists, and found lots to talk about. Mom refused to join in the conversations. She still resented Stoneface's attitude toward us kids. So she would always find other things to do around the place and stay out of the way of the men with their heated denunciations of anyone who did not share their view. Dad was friendly with all the men around the valley. He would talk with Monke and Carlssen, as well as Bill Herman, for long periods when Mom was trying to get him to do some task around the place, so I got saddled with more and more of the heavy chores. It didn't bother me as much as it might have because I was getting proud of my new muscles, and would find opportunities to show off my strength. Quite frankly, I was getting more than a little bit conceited.

Chad came home from school at the end of June and came over. I paused in my never-ending chore of chopping wood and sat down on an upturned block of wood to talk to him.

"Hey, my girl went to Benson's Bridge with me, and I made out with her nearly every day," he told me.

"Aren't you afraid you'd get her pregnant?"

"Naw. That's her problem."

"She might make it yours. How old was she?"

"'Bout fourteen I guess."

"That's underage. We heard about that in school back where we used to live. You could be charged with rape."

"They'd have to prove it was me that done it. She's probably done it with other guys once she done it the first time with me and found out how much fun it was."

"Don't you feel any responsibility?"

"For what? People do it, so what's the big deal? These here bulls fuck the cows all the time. What's the difference?"

I let the subject drop.

Chapter Twenty-Four

I didn't ride with Chad much that summer. Mom insisted that I should stick with Penny, and Chad didn't want to be saddled with a young girl tagging along. If she'd been my age, I'm sure he would have been more interested in her, but I'm equally sure Mom and Dad would put a stop to that if it happened.

I should have been as leery of doing anything else with Chad as Mom was for me. But I guess I'm a sucker. One day, I walked over to the Monke ranch with Chad to say hello to his mom. When Chad was off to school, I didn't see much of Erma Monke, but I liked her, and besides, she was a super cook. The three of us had lunch and talked for a while.

When I was ready to leave to head back to my place, Chad said, "Hey, I got an idea."

"What?"

"You like fishing?"

"Sure."

"Well, Con heard that the fish and game guy is working this here area, looking for poachers. He'll be around early in the morning so's he can catch someone who's out early 'cause they think that's when they won't get caught. Con found out what he's driving, so we can spot him."

"So what?"

"Well, it'd be fun to catch some right under his nose without him spotting us. Hey, if you see his truck, come over and we'll go out and give it a try. It's a brown Ford."

I had a licence, but I knew that none of the Monkes ever bothered with one, and just went out and fished when they wanted to. I couldn't see any point in Chad's scheme, but I'd planned to go fishing to catch some fish for breakfast anyway. The next morning, I took my rod and creel and walked up to the bridge. There was often good fishing under it. A brown pickup was parked nearby. Wondering if this was the fish and game man's truck, I looked for him and thought I saw him sitting in some brush down the creek a ways. Chad called out to me from under the bridge.

"I saw him drive by and stop here. Leave your stuff under the bridge here and we'll sneak down there a ways."

I decided to play along to see what he was up to. The grass was tall and dense and there was brush scattered along the bank of the creek. Chad slithered along through the grass on his belly and I followed. At one point, we could see the man sitting on the opposite bank, looking downstream where the good fishing holes were. When we were still a short distance upstream from him, Chad worked his way over to the bank of the creek, staying behind a clump of bushes. He took out of his pocket a length of black fishing line coiled around a wooden handle. It had a plain hook attached. He had baited it before he came. He gently threw the hook into the stream and let it drift downward to the next pool. After a few minutes, there was a tug on the line and Chad began slowly reeling it in. It took some time, but the fish did not fight very hard and Chad eventually landed it on the bank where we were hiding.

Removing the trout from the hook, he shoved it in the pocket of his jacket.

"I've got more bait. Here, you try it."

"No, I don't want to. Let's get out of here."

"Okay. Hey, that was fun."

He might think so, but I didn't. We edged backward until we had brush between us and the man on the other bank, and then made our way back to the bridge. When we looked back, we saw the man walking back up the creek toward us. I picked up my rod and creel.

"Here, take the fish, Derek." Chad handed it to me and disappeared out into the brush, heading back home. I put the trout into my creel and climbed back up onto the bridge.

The man was waiting for me on the other side. "Been fishing?" he asked.

"Yep."

"Catch anything?"

"Just one. I wanted one for my breakfast."

He walked over and looked into the creel. "Got a licence?"

"Sure do." I reached into my hip pocket and pulled out my wallet, which contained only my student ID card, my fishing licence, and a crumpled five-dollar bill. I extracted my licence and showed it to him.

"Okay, son. Have a nice day." He headed back to his truck, and I let out my breath. He obviously hadn't seen Chad.

It was only as I was walking home that it occurred to me that Chad didn't know I had a licence, and had given me the fish in order to duck the responsibility for his actions, deliberately leaving me holding the bag.

As I walked back toward the T-junction of the roads, a chilling thought literally stopped me in my tracks. I remembered the time the year before when we fell into that open grave, when I had boosted Chad out and expected him to then help hoist me up far enough that I could get a hold on something to pull myself up the rest of the way. Considering Chad's display this morning of leaving me take the rap for his illegal fishing, I thought I probably shouldn't have helped Chad out of the hole and relied on him helping me in return. If I'd had time to think back then, I should have made him help me out first. Once he was out of danger, he might have run off and left me to my fate. He didn't though. He had immediately reached down to give me a hand.

Maybe the difference was that he recognized that getting out of that hole was a life and death problem, but merely getting in trouble over illegal fishing was just sort of a lark.

Chapter Twenty-Five

A few days later the Mounties returned, heading I supposed, to the cabin the 'miners' had used. Several Mounties came and went over the next few days. We hadn't heard any mention of the Beaver Creek murder, as the killing of the young undercover Mountie had been called, all winter or spring. I became more and more curious about what the cops were doing.

Late one afternoon, Sgt. Ross and one other cop, the one who had come with him the year before to take my statement, stopped by our house on their way back from the cabin. It was scorching hot, and both men had damp patches on their shirts from sweat. Mom invited them to stay a while and have some lemonade. They sat at our picnic table outside in the shade of the trees. Mom brought them each a large glass of lemonade and set a pitcher of it on the table. The men gulped it down gratefully and refilled their glasses.

"The water is straight from the spring. It stays cold all summer," she told them as she joined them at the table.

"Really? That's amazing," Ross said. "This is better than ice cubes."

They sat for a while engaging in small talk with Mom while they drank their fill. I wandered over to see what they had to say about the investigation. On seeing me, Sgt. Ross remarked, "Hello Derek. Okay, you should get in on this discussion too. Maybe you'll have some fresh ideas."

"I don't think so. But I'd like to know what you've found out."

"That's what we're here for. I think you folks should know what's going on. You can keep your eyes open for us; be our spotters."

"If we see anything, we'll let you know. You can count on us for that," Mom told them. "So what have you found out so far?"

I wanted to know something too. "What was your guy who got shot doing up here? Was he working, or was he on vacation?"

"He was working, Derek. He was an undercover agent on the drug squad. We've known for some time that shipments of cannabis have been crossing the border into the US at the Arrow border crossing. The border agents on both sides have been on the lookout for it, and we placed a man in Arrow with a drug-sniffing dog."

"Yeah, I saw that dog at the vet's. That's the kind of dog I'd like," I told him.

"Yes, but our K-9 guy can't work twenty-four hours a day. He usually uses the dog during the busy times of day, but he also does his checks at random hours, rather than keeping to a set schedule. But the drugs kept getting across.

"There is an old man named Harry who lives in the next town after Arrow who is a citizens' band radio aficionado. He's been doing it for years. He practically lives at his radio equipment. We know him and trust him, so we asked him to listen to anything that might be related to someone passing a message about a drug shipment. He told us he's heard the occasional brief message that sounds odd to him. Without saying who the message is for, or who is sending it, the speaker (always the same man according to Harry) would make a brief comment that contained something about flowers. One was, 'The flowers are in bloom.' Another was, 'The roses are pretty.' Harry told us there were four of them that he'd heard. He recorded the dates and times he heard them. The dates coincided with the dates when the shipments of cannabis crossed the border.

"So we set up a receiver that could give us a line of direction from the site that was transmitting. We got one contact, and that gave us one line of direction to the site. We needed at least two, preferably three, to pinpoint the site. The one reference we did get only told us that the transmitter is somewhere along a line that goes almost over, but just to the west, of Arrow. We hadn't yet gotten a second bearing, but we sent our guy out to see what he could find in this area. We think he probably found it, and paid for his discovery with his life."

"You don't think it was an accident?" Mom suggested. "I mean, there are often hunting accidents in the woods where we used to live."

"It was no accident, Mrs. Taylor. Our man was shot in the back of the head at close range, and his hands were tied behind his back."

I saw the look of pain on Mom's face. Me, I felt momentarily sick to my stomach.

"We have checked every building around here for a radio transmitter, but we haven't found any."

"You didn't check ours."

"Yes we did, Mrs. Taylor. Your husband let us in. We didn't have a warrant, of course, but most people are cooperative. Mr. Taylor understood why we wanted to know and told us to come in and look if it would help us."

"Oh. He never told me about that. But we do have a radio, and there's no antenna. And all the other people who live here in the valley have radios."

"Household radios are only receivers. They have built-in antennas. You can get antennas to put up outside to improve reception if you want. But that's not what we're looking for. We're looking for a transmitter. And it would need a tall antenna in order to transmit anywhere outside this valley."

"Like you have on your cars," I said.

"That's right, Derek. But it would probably be quite a lot taller."

"So what's your new interest?" Mom, who is a sort of matter-of-fact person, directed them back to the important subject.

"The radio calls have started again, and so have the cross-border shipments. This year it's not flowers though. This year the code word seems to be the names of shoe manufacturers. So far, it's been Nike and Reebok. But Harry, the old guy who listens to the traffic on CB radio, is sure the person making the calls is the same one as last year. Harry is very good at recognizing voices. He even wrote a book about it—short stories he dreamed up from imagining the type of person making the various radio calls he's heard. The stories are a lot of fun to read. That guy is a genius in his own way."

"Does he often give other information to you?"

"He does when there's an emergency or he thinks there is something suspicious about a call."

"Like what?" I asked.

"Sometimes it's something simple, like the time he heard a child's voice making a distress call, but he heard giggling in the background. He talked to the child long enough to get an idea of where the child was calling from. Then he phoned us and we went to the address and read the riot act to the child and his parents. Another time, Harry listened in on what he thought sounded like a couple of guys planning a robbery. We were waiting for the guys when they arrived at the business they planned to rob."

"Wow. That's neat."

Ross leaned forward, his expression getting serious.

"Derek, when you and your sister are out riding, if you see any radio antenna, note where it is, but get away pronto from the place you spotted it. Don't tell anyone but your family, and let your dad contact us when he goes to town. Don't put yourself in danger. I don't mean to scare you, and chances are, if you see an antenna, and someone is there using a radio, they'll just think you and your sister are just kids out riding your horses and not bother about it. But just to be safe, leave the area immediately and don't let anyone except your parents know that you spotted it."

"Do you still think the radio is over near Arrow?"

"Yes, we do, but we've set up our receiver again and are trying to get another line to cross the one we already have, in order to pinpoint the spot where the transmitter is. Once we get that, we'll be able to do a thorough search of the area."

"You don't think the guys who are using it have moved their transmitter? I mean, I'd think that they might want a new place if they thought you might know where the old one was."

"That's a possibility we have to keep in mind."

"We haven't ever ridden out to the east, toward the town," I explained. "We mainly go the other way, down the creek, now. Penny thought the area up there by the cabin was creepy that day we stopped by and talked to you, and we don't want to go there any more. But I'll keep an eye out for an antenna," I promised. "I'm pretty sure there's no antenna down where we've ridden. I know that area pretty well, but I'll keep watching, even down there. Maybe we'll ride up to the east, too.

"Good."

Mom was frowning. "If you pulled out all the pot plants last year, and those guys moved out, why are they at it again?"

"We think they must have another grow-op somewhere. And we know that there are local people involved."

"So they might have moved their radio to the new area, don't you think?"

"They might. Or it may be in the same place because that's near where the man who makes the calls lives or works."

"Where did those guys go to?" I wanted to know.

"Do you mean the men who lived in the cabin?"

"Yeah."

"We think they went back to the States. They're American."

"So you know who they are." Mom remarked.

"They signed for that mining claim, so we knew who was living up there before we showed up. We have contacted the police in all the northwestern states, as well as BC and Alberta. We've checked on them and we think they would go to an area with forests. They're former loggers. They cleaned out that cabin completely when they left. They didn't leave a single scrap that could point to them. They must have packed up once they had killed our man, and left as soon as they buried the body."

I didn't think so, but I didn't say anything. When I saw those guys up there at the cabin that night, they were relaxed and sitting in front of their cabin drinking beer. They must have been waiting for the moon to come up so they could see to bury the guy without using a light, in case anyone drove by on the road. I think that it was our tripping the alarm that caused them to hurry up and leave, because they'd know that someone had spotted their grow-op. I'd been wondering since the cops first came by our place, where those guys had stashed the body before they buried it. What if we had stumbled across it? What if it had already been in the grave and we had fallen in on top of it? Every time I thought about it, it sent a shiver up my spine.

But there was something else that bothered me.

"If your guy went out with Con, how'd he get back up there to the grow-op?"

"That's something we're puzzled about. He must have spotted something before he left, and after he parked his car in Arrow, he went back again to check it out. There are trails up the cliff from Arrow. You need to be fit, but not necessarily a mountain climber, to come up from the town. Or else someone in town drove him back out here to the valley. You probably wouldn't have noticed a car or pickup that you thought was local. We are pretty sure those guys had at least one confederate living either in town or in this area."

"Are you sure your guy left the valley in the first place? Couldn't someone else have driven his car into town?"

"We know Con Monke brought him out of the mountains. Mrs. Herman was working in her garden and saw them go by."

"Oh." It didn't fit, I thought. "But…"

"What's on your mind, son?"

"But Con didn't bring him out," I insisted. "Con didn't bring anyone out of the mountains on Friday afternoon. I was sitting up looking out over the meadow on Friday night. It was real clear in the moonlight. That's why I wanted to go riding on Saturday night. Anyway, I saw Con coming home with his pack string, way late that night, and there wasn't anybody with him. He was leading the other saddle horse and his packhorses. I watched them for quite a while."

That got everyone's attention. Mom asked, "Are you sure Grace Herman saw them Friday afternoon? I know she wouldn't lie, but could she have been mistaken? Maybe she saw them going up into the mountains earlier and just got the two times mixed up."

"Is Mrs. Herman reliable about other things?"

"Yes, she is. I don't know what to think, but if you're going to ask if I trust Derek's memory, yes, I do."

"Well, maybe Monke brought our man out in the afternoon and had to go back later to get some other stuff."

"But why did Con have the extra saddle horse with him that night?" I asked.

"It's a problem, but I'm sure we'll find the answer. At any rate, it seems pretty clear that our man did come out of the mountains Friday afternoon and did drive his car into town."

I still wasn't convinced and I sat there frowning as the Mounties thanked Mom and got up to leave. Mom stopped them with one more question.

"You don't seem to think that we are the local people in this drug-smuggling ring. Why not?"

"It was going on for some time before you moved out here, Mrs. Taylor. Besides we did check your background."

Mom got red in the face. "Oh."

Chapter Twenty-Six

One evening I was working with a kit that was designed to teach its users about electricity. I bought it, with money from my allowance, on our most recent trip to Caribou. I was trying to make a doorbell for our house. We didn't really need a doorbell, because everyone in the valley just walked in and out of each other's houses. No one locked their doors. At least, no one except Old Stoneface.

I had my supplies, which included a bundle of pre-cut wires in different colours according to their length, set out on a small table in the living room. I had to go do something for Mom, and when I got back, the bundle of wires was gone. Old Stoneface had come over and was sitting in the living room talking to Dad, but when I returned from helping Mom, he was gone. I knew he had taken my wires and complained to Dad.

"Don't ever let me hear you say anything like that again," Dad upbraided me. "Stone is a perfectly nice man. He wouldn't engage in petty thieving."

"Then who took my wires?"

"You must have put them somewhere."

"No, I didn't. They were right there." I pointed adamantly at a spot on the tabletop. "Did you take them?"

"Derek! Don't ever say that to me again."

"They were here and now they're not. So where are they?" My voice was rising, not only in intensity, but in pitch, from baritone to tenor. It still did that occasionally when I got excited or angry.

"Shut up. I don't want another word out of you. Go help your mother."

I gathered the rest of the kit into its box and ran up the ladder to my bedroom, fuming at the unfairness of Dad's tirade.

Old Stoneface turned up at our place a few days later. I hoped he was bringing me back my bundle of wires, since I couldn't continue with my project until I had some wires. But no such luck. He barely glanced at me and addressed himself to Mom, Dad not being home at the time.

He asked Mom, "Do you by any chance have a spare heavy duty padlock I could borrow until I can buy one? The combination lock on my workshop got very corroded over the winter and even though I've used WD40 on it several times, I'm still having a lot of trouble opening it. I'm afraid I'll lock myself out of my workshop if I keep trying to use it."

"As a matter of fact, I think we do," Mom replied. She found a suitable lock on a pantry shelf devoted to tools. The key had been left in the lock so it wouldn't get lost. She handed it to Stoneface.

"There should be two keys," Old Stoneface said in what I thought was an accusing manner. He was like that on the rare occasions he actually talked to Mom. It was obvious to me that he considered women to be inferior and that they should do the bidding of men.

"I think it must have gotten lost," Mom explained. "I couldn't find a second key when I unpacked after we moved into the house. We left stuff in storage while we were living in the tent."

"Would you look for it please?" Stoneface asked gruffly.

It was obvious that Mom was fuming at the man's gall, but she rummaged around through all the drawers that she thought an odd small object might have been tossed into.

The search was unsuccessful. I was watching her with anxiety, as I had suddenly seen the way to get into Old Stoneface's workshop. I knew where the key was. I remember that the keys had dropped on the floor when Mom was unpacking a box of odds and ends. She had found one key, but the other had skittered under a chair. I'd picked up the spare key and put it in my pocket because I was busy doing something else at the time. Later, I tossed it in a drawer, but not one Mom was now looking through. It should still be there.

But did I tell Mom that I knew where the missing key was? Not on your life! I had other plans for that key.

To my relief, Mom gave up her search. Stoneface left, grumbling that he'd have to put up with having only one key, as if it was our fault that he wasn't being given the spare one.

Later that afternoon, when no one was looking, I went to the drawer I'd tossed the key into, and rummaged around to see if it was still there. It was. I slipped it into the pocket of my jeans. The key seemed to burn a hole in my pocket as I started making plans for my invasion of Old Stoneface's fortress. It knew that I'd have to do something quickly, before he went to town and bought a new padlock.

Chapter Twenty-Seven

My opportunity came two days later.

I was chopping wood. Yes, again. Chopping wood took up an overwhelming amount of my time. We spent the summer skidding in more dead trees and sawing them into firewood lengths, which we then had to be split into large chunks and stacked on two sides of the woodshed, north and west, to form a windbreak to keep snow from blowing in. The house sheltered the woodshed on the south side, and east winds weren't very common.

There is a saying that chopping wood warms you twice. That's true, but unfortunately most of the chopping occurs during the summer when warming yourself is not a preferred way of spending your time. And in the winter, you only venture outside in the bitter cold to split the large chunks into stove-sized pieces when you absolutely have to.

Anyway, I was chopping wood when I saw Old Stoneface's SUV go by our house and turn up the road toward town. Uh, oh, I thought, That meant that he'll probably buy a new padlock while he was there, so I'd better get a move on if I wanted to get into his workroom before he got back. I dropped the axe and ran into the house to change clothes. I was wearing jeans and heavy work boots. I needed loose comfortable clothes and shoes. I threw on shorts, a T-shirt, and sneakers, and grabbed the spare key to the padlock.

Penny stuck her head up over the top of the ladder to our loft. "Whatcha doing?" she asked.

"None of your business," I replied hoping to scare her away.

"Hey! You're always going off and doing mysterious things, and you never take me along. I want to get in on the interesting stuff, too."

"Well, I don't need you tagging along." I motioned to her to get off the ladder, but Penny held her ground. "Move over. I want by."

"Not till you tell me where you're going."

"Over to Old Stoneface's, and I don't want you along. I don't need a little sister with me. It's dangerous."

"Are you going to break in?"

"No, but I'm going to find out what's in his shop."

"How're you going to get in?"

I rolled my eyes. I knew I couldn't get rid of her without telling her what I was about to do. I pulled the spare key to the padlock we had loaned our neighbour out of my pocket and held it under her nose. "I'm going to unlock the door and walk in. Now get out of my way."

"Is that the spare key Mom was looking for? Where'd you get it?"

"I knew where it was. Now move."

"And you didn't tell Mom? Hey, big brother, that's neat. I'll go with you and act as your lookout. You'll need one to let you know when Old Stoneface comes back. If he finds you there, he'll skin you alive. You need me. I'll make a great lookout for you."

I saw the eager look on her face and knew I wasn't going to be able to brush her off. Maybe she could help me after all. I gave in. "Okay. Come along."

We ran across the pasture, rolled under the bottom strand of barbed wire, and scrambled over the rocky outcrops, avoiding the gullies in between in order to make time. When we descended from the last outcrop, we were just outside Old Stoneface's fence. I called a halt and looked around.

"Come with me," I said as I walked back up to the top of the last rock outcrop. "You stay here. You can see the road from the Monke ranch all the way across the bridge. Keep down behind these bushes, because I'd just as soon no one saw us out here. Don't watch me. Keep your eyes on the road all the time. If you see his car, give a whistle."

Penny had a very penetrating whistle, which she used to call her horse, who always came running, since Penny rewarded him with either carrots or grain when he came to her. Mom complained that she had to buy more carrots for the animals than for us to eat. We got them in big bags.

I went on, "If you miss him when he's on that part of the road, but see him on this road, closer, give two quick whistles, as loud as you can."

"Okay. I can do that. Trust me." She took her position on the top of the outcrop, behind the brush, looking toward the Monke ranch where she could see any vehicle coming down into the valley. I took off at a run to the edge of the creek where Stone's fence extended into the water. I waded around the lower end of the fence and back to dry land, water squishing out of my sneakers. Then taking a deep breath, I set out on my first criminal adventure.

I ran up the slope toward the workshop, rounded the corner, and stopped at the door. Our padlock was there all right. I felt the key in my pocket. I hesitated. I knew that what I was about to do was illegal. I'd been brought up to obey the law, to be honest in all my dealings.

But Old Stoneface had stolen from me. I was just going to retrieve my own stolen property, I told myself. Okay, that was not the whole truth and nothing but the truth. I could not push down the thought that retrieving my property was not the primary reason for my being here. I had, for over a year, yearned to get inside that workshop to see what the mean old man was doing in there. The theft of my wires was only a convenient excuse. Could I reconcile my desire to find out what he was up to with my moral upbringing?

Well, the guy was mean, he was a thief, and I wasn't going to do him any harm. I was just going to look around. I wouldn't take anything other than my wires, if I could find them.

But in the end, the most convincing argument I had was that I knew I'd kick myself if I chickened out now.

I reached for the padlock.

Chapter Twenty-Eight

The lock was tilted up from the hasp, leaning toward the left. He probably left it that way so he could tell if anyone had meddled with it, I thought. So I reasoned that I'd better remember exactly how it was sitting, so I could leave it that way when I went out.

Another thought struck me. What if the key I was holding wasn't really the spare key to that lock? It would give me an out, but it would be a major disappointment.

I inserted the key. It turned easily, and the lock clicked open. Okay, Derek, I told myself, now you have to go through with it.

I pushed the door open and stepped inside. The building seemed to be a combination shop and office. The place was spotlessly clean, the hinges on the door well oiled. Everything seemed to be in a carefully planned place. Tools hung on a rack on the wall. Secretarial supplies were neatly arranged on a desk. A list of addresses stood in a holder on the desk. Stoneface appeared to be a tidy, well-organized man.

I took a look at the addresses. There were five on the list. The first three names looked vaguely familiar, but the addresses under them did not. These names and addresses had a line carefully drawn through them. The last two names did not look familiar at all. I tried to remember where I had seen those crossed-out names before, but couldn't.

I didn't have any more time to waste trying to remember because Old Stoneface could come back at any minute, so I moved over to a workbench where he was apparently assembling something. Beside the partly finished device was a padded mailer, with an address label on it, and on the label was the fourth name and address from the list. The address label also had a logo and name of what I took to be a business. Stoneface had a business that he didn't want anyone to know too much about. So that was it. Mystery solved. As simple as that. The list was of customers who had ordered something from Stoneface. I was disappointed, until I looked more closely at what he was making.

Whatever devise he was putting together, he was using, I noticed, a couple of wires from my electricity set. I was right; he had stolen them. But where were the rest of the wires? Not on the bench top. In a drawer? One drawer was not quite closed. I reached for the handle, but thought better of it. If I pulled out the drawer, I'd leave fingerprints. I took the key, which I had removed from the padlock and put in my pocket, and slid it through the crack left by the partially open drawer. Using the key as a lever, I pulled open the drawer. There were my wires, the whole bundle of them, minus of course, the ones being used in Stoneface's project. I grabbed the bundle and stuck it in a pocket of my shorts. I pushed the drawer shut, again using the key, and trying to get it shut just enough so that there was the same tiny crack.

I went back to the list. I didn't pay any more attention to the three crossed-off names, but instead concentrated my attention on memorizing the last two, the one on the label and the fifth name, not yet used. I have a good visual memory for printed numbers and words, a talent I had tried to improve upon when Penny was showing off her own memory skills.

Penny's piercing whistle sounded loud to my attentive ears and broke my concentration. Time to go. Just a little more work on memorizing the names and addresses to make sure I got them right. But then her second whistle sounded even louder than the first. I dashed for the door.

Remembering to place the lock cocked up to the left, I paused to be sure it was right, but it fell back to the normal hanging position. It also hadn't quite latched, and sprung open again. I reached for it, my hand shaking in my anxiety to get out of there. Then I remembered fingerprints. I would have left them all over the lock. I grabbed a fistful of grass and rubbed the lock, put it in the cocked-up position again, and blew off the grass particles.

Penny whistled again—twice. What I'd done had to be enough. I turned and ran, plunging into the water and splashing around the fence. I threw myself to the ground as I saw Old Stoneface's SUV turn into his driveway. He didn't stop to close his gate, but walked purposefully toward the workshop. While he was briefly hidden behind the house, I ran toward the gully. It was the one with the blackberry bush, now covered with berries. Penny had scrambled over the next rocky outcrop and was peering over the top.

"Be careful," she warned, her voice low and urgent. She didn't need to tell me that, and I wondered why she had bothered. I soon found out.

The outcrop closest to Stone's cabin shelved gently down to the water's edge, and even in the gully on the other side of it, I was still visible to anyone looking out from the cabin. With my white T-shirt, I could be easily seen if I remained where I was. I dived into the blackberry bush. It was an old-fashioned bramble, with wicked thorns. I was willing to brave being ripped by those thorns if only I could get myself out of sight. Next time I did a little burglary, I swore to myself, I'd wear dull-coloured clothes—and rubber gloves.

But thorns weren't the only hazard the bramble held. I dived headlong into a hornet's nest. I backed hastily out, batting wildly at the hornets that were attacking every bare piece of flesh. I had to get out of there, but looking up I could see Old Stoneface turning away from the door to his shop—turning toward me. I threw myself back into the berry bush. By now, the hornets, thoroughly aroused, were out in force. They swarmed my head. I backed out, flailing at the beasts, brushing them out of my hair. But the thought of being in full view of Old Stoneface who, once he realized that someone had been in his shop, would be out for my blood if he saw me nearby, made me stay in the outer part of the bramble bush.

My predicament reminded me of how one day, we had been burning brush, and a mouse, which had apparently made it's nest in the brush, dashed out into the open to get away from the fire. Mowser, who had followed us, saw the mouse and rushed to pounce on it. The mouse reversed course and ran back into the burning brush, only to emerge again as the flames got closer. Mowser attacked again, but I grabbed him just before he reached the mouse, which was retreating into the fire again. The mouse ran to safety. I was sure Mowser would undoubtedly catch the mouse in another day or two, but I couldn't stand to see the poor creature having to decide which way it would prefer to die.

Now I was in the same sort of danger. From her hiding place atop the rock outcropping, Penny had a better view of the situation. She told me later that she saw Stoneface go to his back door and fit his key into the lock. Knowing that he wouldn't be looking in our direction for several seconds at least, she called out urgently, "Run!"

I ran! Down to the water's edge, where I dived into the creek and swam upstream, underwater, for as long as I could hold my breath. It was a calm pool where the water flowed sluggishly, so I managed to swim quite a ways before I was forced to surface. When I came up, I was blessedly free of the angry hornets. Penny, now in the second gully upstream, waded up to her knees into the creek and reached out a hand to help me make my way to shore.

"You should have seen yourself back there, batting away at those hornets. Did they sting you?"

"Of course they stung me," I snapped. "All over my head and everything."

"Your eye is swelling shut."

"I know my eye is swelling shut. You don't have to tell me."

"Okay, don't freak out about it. I think we'd better wade through the creek rather than climbing over the rocks."

Penny seemed to have assumed the guidance of the expedition, taking over from her wounded leader. She peered over the top of the next outcrop and reported that Old Stoneface must be in the house now, so we could move. "And I don't see him looking out the window. Let's go."

We waded as far as our pasture fence, crawled under the wire and trudged up toward the house.

"So that key must have been the right one. You got in okay," Penny said.

"Yeah, it was."

"What'd you do in there?"

I pulled out the bundle of wires, grinning as I waved them under her nose. Penny knew that I thought Old Stoneface had taken them. "Reclaiming my property."

"See. You did need me along," Penny reminded me smugly. "You'd have been caught in there if I hadn't been on the lookout, and he might have murdered you."

"You weren't a very good lookout, though," I retorted. "You let him get too close before you warned me.

"No I didn't. I saw him when he first passed the Monkes' place, and I whistled. But then I saw that he was driving real fast, so I whistled again. When you didn't come out of that shop, I thought you hadn't heard me, so I whistled again."

"I heard you, but I was real busy."

"Busy doing what?"

"Memorizing names on a list."

"Why didn't you just take the list if it was so important?"

"Because then he would really know someone had been in there."

"He's going to know, anyway, when he can't find those wires. But maybe he'll think he just misplaced them. Same with the list if you took it."

"Not that guy. You should have seen that place. That guy is really organized. He has a place for everything, and everything in its place. He'll spot everything that's missing right away."

"Then, if he knows that someone took those wires, he'll know it was you."

"But he won't dare do anything about it, because he stole them from me in the first place. But if I took anything else, he'd come looking for it. Look, don't tell anybody about this. Can I trust you?"

"Of course you can. What do you think I am, anyway? I'm glad you've gotten even with that guy. I can't stand him. But what's so important about this list you were memorizing?"

"That's my private business and I'm not going to tell you."

She looked for a minute as if she might argue with me about that, but apparently changed her mind. Instead, she said, "Maybe you should throw that key away. If you throw it in the creek, no one will ever find it. You don't want to be caught with it on you.

I'd been thinking the same thing. But when I pulled the key out of my pocket, I changed my mind.

"I don't think so. I might want to get in there again, especially if I can't remember those last two names and addresses."

Penny frowned. "Well, be sure you hide it really, really well. You don't want anyone to find it.

I had to admit to myself that Penny was right. And if she hadn't gone with me to be my sentinel, I would have definitely been in big trouble. I had assumed that Old Stoneface was going into Arrow when I saw him leave, but he must have only gone over the divide to the mailboxes where the road to Beaver Creek turns off from the road up the river.

Maybe, I decided, it isn't so bad after all to let my little sister go places with me.

Chapter Twenty-Nine

We squished through the kitchen, leaving wet footprints. Mom saw me and demanded, "What have you been doing? You must have been in the creek."

We found a blackberry bush and I wanted to get some berries, but there was a hornets' nest in it and they came after me. I had to dive into the creek to get away from them." Making up fat lies to cover up something I didn't want to talk about was getting easier all the time. Practice makes perfect. Besides, it wasn't a complete lie anyway.

"What happened to your eye?" It was now about half-shut.

"One of the hornets stung me there."

"Well, get out of your wet clothes while I see what we've got in the medicine chest that might help."

Good. No more questions.

I scrambled up the ladder to my bedroom, and got out of my wet clothes and into the jeans I had been wearing earlier. I dried my hands carefully, found a sheet of paper and a pen, and tried to dredge up the two names from the list I'd seen in the shop that I wanted to write down before I forgot them. Fortunately, the names were not weird foreign ones so I got those down okay. The addresses were harder and I don't think I got them exactly correct, but I was close enough that they could be looked up for correct spelling of the street names, and I was pretty sure I got the street numbers right. I was good at remembering numbers. I folded the paper twice and hid it in the bottom of one of my clothes drawers, along with the key.

When I came back down the ladder, Mom had our first aid kit open. She found a nearly empty bottle of calamine lotion, and handed it to me. "Here, put this on your skin. Don't waste any. That's all we've got." I dabbed the lotion on stings on my arms and legs. There wasn't enough to do my head.

Dad and Bill Herman came in the door, and Mom called out, "Bill would you go home and ask Grace if she has any calamine lotion, or something like it? Derek got tangled up in a hornets' nest and we've put calamine on the stings, but we ran out."

Bill dashed to his truck, and fifteen minutes later, he reappeared. "She doesn't have any of that stuff, but she says to find a fir tree and cut open some of those blisters on it, and squeeze out the balsam to put on the stings."

"Oh, that's right," Mom exclaimed. "They're called balsam firs."

"That's them. I hope it works."

"I know where there's a big fir tree. I'll go with you," Penny volunteered.

"Wait a minute," Mom commanded. "I want Derek to take an antihistamine first."

Mom had packed a number of over-the-counter remedies when we moved out here. Antihistamine was one of them. She peered at the label. "Hmm. I guess Derek can be considered an adult now. He's big enough. You can have two of these." She shook two tablets out into her hand while I got a glass of water. I swallowed the pills.

Penny dashed away and I followed. We found the tree, and I pulled out my penknife and started slitting the tiny blisters. It took a lot of them to get enough balsam to dab on all the stings. I worked on my arms and legs, while Penny did all the stings on the top of my head. "You'll never get all this stuff out of your hair, you know. You'll have to shave your head." She laughed. "You'll look like an old man, all bald."

"Don't laugh at me. It isn't funny."

"But it is," she said, laughing even louder.

The balsam may have made a sticky mess, but it sure worked. As soon as balsam was dabbed on a spot, the pain went away. It seemed miraculous.

By the time we got back to the house, I was getting drowsy from the antihistamine. Penny and I had hammocks slung between trees and we slept there on hot summer nights. It got pretty hot up there in our loft, so most nights, we slept outside in the hammocks until the night-time chill was well established, then moved back inside. I headed for my hammock, rolled in, and fell asleep almost immediately.

When I woke up later, I heard Mom and Dad talking. They were sitting at the picnic table and I could hear them clearly.

"What's with Derek? He keeps falling into the creek," Dad griped. "That's at least half a dozen times he's come in dripping wet."

"That's just Derek. He's a boy. Didn't you ever do things like that when you were a boy?"

"I don't remember ever falling into a creek, or river, or swimming pool or anything like that."

I didn't think his complaint was fair. I'd only come home dripping wet five times. And Penny had been with me three of those times. I didn't hear Dad complain about her. Then I wondered what he would have thought if he'd known about the other place I'd fallen into! I wasn't about to tell him *that* story. I wasn't even going to tell Penny.

When I woke up from my antihistamine-induced sleep the next morning, I did the last thing I needed to do as a result of my adventure into crime. I now remembered where I had seen, in a newspaper article, the three names Old Stoneface had crossed off his list. If it had been in a newspaper, it was probably now tacked to my ceiling.

There was one chance in four that it would be on the outside of one of the double sets of paper, that is if it had not been used for starting a fire in the cook stove. I thought that it was fairly recently that I read the article, so it should be on the most recent area of the ceiling that I had covered. The swelling below my eye had receded, so I could read with no problem.

I didn't find the article, but I found another one that caught my attention. In my mind's eye, I saw Dad reading the paper at the dinner table, holding it up so it wouldn't rest on dirty plates that had not yet been cleared off the table. It was my turn to clear the table and do the dishes, so any way to procrastinate was welcome. Reading the paper was something Mom encouraged me to do, so this was as good a diversion as anything. I could read the backside from where I sat opposite Dad.

He was complaining, as usual, about the monotony of the news. The article he was reading, he told us, was another one about a young woman going missing while hitchhiking on a notorious northern British Columbia road dubbed the Highway of Tears. The article I had read on the reverse side of the missing woman one was the one I was now searching for.

I was in luck. There on my ceiling was the Highway of Tears article.

I loosened the tacks holding that page of the newspaper and carefully took down the sheet. When I turned it over, I found the article I had read at the kitchen table. My memory hadn't failed me. The three names on Old Stoneface's list were mentioned in it.

Now I knew what he was up to. But what could I do about it, isolated out here in this valley?

Chapter Thirty

It was a week before Dad went into town. Mom asked me to go with him. She gave me a list of items needed to replenish our medicine chest, calamine lotion being one of the items. "And ask the pharmacist what would be best for bee or hornet stings," she added. "Something less sticky that the stuff from those fir tree blisters." The balsam from the fir tree had hardened and, as Penny so laughingly predicted, was impossible to wash out of my hair. Mom took a device for cutting hair she brought with us when we moved and nearly scalped me. What was left of my wavy brown hair was not enough to protect my scalp from the sun, so I now had sunburn on the top of my head, which was almost as bad as the hornet stings. I wore my cowboy hat everywhere to protect me from further sunburn. I needed a baseball cap, and mentally added it to Mom's list.

At the drug store in town, Dad handed me a small key and told me to go to the mailbox, which was in the back corner of the drugstore, and get the mail while he picked up the faxes that the store was holding for him. He sat down in a chair to read the faxes as I riffled through the mail. I found one envelope that looked like a business letter, and another from Dad's financial advisor. I gave those envelopes to Dad, and walked over to the pharmacy counter. I waited for the pharmacist, whose name, according to the sign on the door was Evans, to finish with another customer. Dad opened his mail. When he looked at his financial statement, he gave a dejected groan. Then he opened the other envelope and read the letter it contained. Something in it sent him into a rage.

He leapt to his feet, and slammed the papers in his hand onto a table nearby, making the items displayed on it jump.

"Of all the idiotic crap, this takes the cake!" he raged, causing everyone in the store to turn toward him in amazement. He interrupted the pharmacist to say, "I've got to go get a letter written. I'll be back as soon a Marge can get it typed for me. I'll have to send it, so I'll pay you then." Marge was the local lady who had agreed to type letters for him.

"All right, Mr. Taylor." the druggist replied soothingly in his English accent. "Take your time."

Dad stomped out of the store.

The pharmacist finished with his other customer, looked at me and said, "Now, young Master Taylor, what can I do for you?"

I was tickled at being addressed so formally. I brought out Mom's list. "We need these things for our medicine kit, Mr. Evans. Especially the calamine. Mom used it all up when I got stung by hornets. She gave me a couple of antihistamine pills, too. She wants to know what you have for stings." I told him about my swollen eye and the other welts on my head, arms, and legs. I also told him about using the balsam from the fir trees when we ran out of calamine.

He walked with me around the store, finding the items on Mom's list and ending with some ointment he said would help take the pain out of stings. "Your mom acted sensibly," he said, "but this should be even better."

"Actually, it was a neighbour who told me to put the stuff from blisters on fir trees on the stings, and it worked better than anything else. But I don't suppose you'd approve of any old remedy like that."

"You're wrong there, young man. I would definitely approve. I've heard several people swear by fir balsam as a treatment for mosquito bites. And balsam is used as a base for soothing, healing ointments."

"Yeah, balsam is what she called it."

"Actually, many of our common drugs were originally made from plants commonly found in nature. ASA, or Aspirin which is its trade name, was first extracted from willow bark. Atropine comes from the belladonna plant and digitalis from the foxglove."

"What are those?"

"Have you ever had eye drops used to dilate your pupils?"

"No, but Mom did. She couldn't drive home until it wore off."

"That was atropine. It has many other uses as well. Digitalis is a heart drug. Then there's penicillin. It used to be extracted from a kind of mould similar to the one that grows on stale bread."

"Wow. I didn't know that. That's really interesting."

"By the way, if you ever have a more severe allergic reaction and it swells up a lot, you should come here right away, and I can give you an epinephrine injection."

"What's that?"

"Adrenalin. That's a trade name. Epinephrine is the scientific name."

"Are you allowed to do that?"

"Yes, I am. I'm a paramedic, and this store is the local first-aid station. I would also call a doctor who could tell me whether I should send you on to a hospital. I can give 'first responder' care and call an ambulance if necessary. So stop here first; don't drive all the way to Caribou. Can you remember to tell your parents? They need to know."

"Sure thing, Mr. Evans, but what if your store is closed?"

He pointed toward the ceiling. "I live upstairs."
"Hey, thanks for telling me all this stuff. I'll tell Mom."

Dad hadn't returned by the time I had everything on Mom's list, so I went down the street to the general store. Looking around, I spotted a display of caps. There were ones with logos, ones with catchy sayings, ones with animals, and plain ones of every conceivable colour. Prominently displayed were Toronto Blue Jays caps, and because the US is right across the border, Seattle Mariners caps. Which should I get? I eventually settled on a red cap with a maple leaf. Might as well be patriotic. There was a light blue one with a caricature of a cat that I knew Penny would love. Maybe I should buy it for her. I counted the money that remained after I had paid the drug store, and then decided that I should buy Penny's cap out of my own money so it would be a gift from me, not part of the family's clothing budget.

Penny and I had an allowance back in the States, and it had been continued when we moved up here, even though we didn't have any opportunity to spend it. The money accumulated over time, so Penny and I opened small savings accounts at the local bank. We did spend part of it whenever we went to Caribou, but mainly what I would have liked to buy was stuff I couldn't use out here because we had no electricity or computer.

I paid for my cap, put it on my head, threw my cowboy hat into the pickup, and crossed the street to the bank. I took enough out of my savings to buy Penny's cap and went back to the general store.

I checked, but Dad still had not returned to the drug store, so I walked down toward the vet clinic. Looking toward the border crossing, I saw the Mountie who was the handler of Jet, the drug-sniffing dog, walking along a line of cars waiting to cross the border. Jet was walking quietly along with his handler. Apparently no one was trying to smuggle drugs today. When they had passed all the cars waiting to enter the US, the man and dog crossed the road and walked along the ones lined up at Canadian Customs, which was closer to town than the US Customs building. Still nothing aroused the dog's interest.

Seeing the Mountie made me think of Sgt. Ross's request that I keep an eye out for a radio antenna while out riding. I realized that, except for the time Penny and I rode up to the miners' cabin, I had only explored the terrain downstream from our house. Chad always led off in that direction. I suggested to him at one time that we ride up toward the cliff that overlooked the town, but he told me there was nothing up that way worth seeing. "It's all clear-cuts," he said.

Maybe I should ride that way for a change anyway. I really wanted to find that antenna and be able to report another clue to Sgt. Ross. His warning that it could be dangerous didn't bother me.

One of these days maybe I'd learn to take advice on avoiding danger seriously.

Chapter Thirty-One

Dad was in a foul mood all the way home. I was upset that he didn't want to stop at the café before leaving Arrow. I was counting on doing so. He wasn't in any mood for arguing, so I kept my mouth shut and just let him stew. As a result, he took it out on Mom when we got home. There was tension in the air for a week.

In the mail, there were letters for Penny, Mom, and me, from our maternal grandmother. I decided to wait until I got home to read mine. Before I gave Penny her letter, I gave her the cap with the weird cat on it. She was delighted and actually kissed me when I told her I'd bought it with my own money. She wore it all the time until late fall when warmer caps were required. Then I gave her the letter. She and I read our letters eagerly, exchanging bits of news as we did so. Mom waited until evening to read hers, and when she read it I could see her relax and smile. For a few moments we all forgot the problems caused by Dad's anger. When she finished the letter, I told her about my conversation with the pharmacist.

"I'm relieved to hear that," she said. "At least I know that when something happens to us out here, we don't have to just lie down and die." Months later, I would remember that comment.

Over the next few days, Penny and I used any excuse we could find to get away from the house, of course after diligently doing our chores so as not to give Dad the opportunity to yell at us. I knew that what was bothering him had something to do with finances, and I also knew that the financial statements he had received showed that the mortgage crisis in the US had caused Dad's investments to lose a third of their value.

Penny and I always fled when he started in on one of his rants, and I figured that now would be as good time as any to ride up in the hills to the east, the direction I had never taken before. Penny was willing to go along as well, but I didn't tell her about my motive for riding in that direction. I merely said I'd never ridden that way before, and was curious about what was there. Penny said she had, but never very far, and had always stayed in sight of the valley.

My new adventure had to be put off when a spate of rain descended upon us. It was welcome after the hot dry summer days. There would still be plenty of summer left to enjoy our ride once the rain stopped.

About a week after that trip to town, I was just falling asleep one night, when I was aroused by Dad's yelling, and Mom telling him, "Keep your voice down. You'll wake the kids."

Mom's tone could be very forceful when she was angry and was trying to keep her temper under control. Dad obediently lowered his voice. I was intrigued, so I got out of bed and crept over to the top of the ladder where I could hear them talking in the living room.

"First, it was the damned investments going sour, then that letter from Hollins. I should have sold the investments last winter when they started to fall."

"How were you to know? And don't even think of selling now. We can't help it if American securities are falling in value. I don't understand all this nonsense about sub-prime mortgages, but everyone's investments are taking a hit, here in Canada as well as in the US. So no, now is not the time to sell."

"If I don't, they might go down to nothing."

"No they won't. This isn't like the Depression when all the banks failed. We need to wait it out. Eventually, they'll come back again."

"You don't understand, Liz. We need something to live on."

"Don't tell me I don't understand." Mom's voice became steely hard. "I probably know more about what we need to pay the bills than you do. It's not the investments that are causing the problem now. It's that we need some income."

"That's what I'm telling you, Liz. Hollins isn't going to send work to me any more." Dad was having trouble keeping his voice down.

"Well, what are you going to do about it?"

"I sent them back a letter and told them what I thought of them. I've done good work for them. They should treat me with more respect."

"*That* wasn't a very good idea, Phil. If you want them to still send you work, you shouldn't have gotten them mad at you."

"They needed to know what I thought."

"You should have waited to answer their letter until you calmed down, and you should have given some thought about how to word your reply. You're good at telling other people how to express themselves. You should have taken your own advice."

Hollins Publishing was a publisher of a number of technical journals and company newsletters. Dad didn't actually work for them; he was one of their free-lance editors. When one of the journals received an article and liked the ideas expressed in it, but not the way they were written, they would send the article to Dad for him to work with the author, or more commonly, the authors, to get it into acceptable language and structure for publication. Dad wasn't the only free-lance editor who worked for Hollins, but he was used frequently, and he had come to rely on the income he received.

The authors paid Dad directly. They were often slow in paying, but Dad would remind them that he wouldn't send the article to the publisher until he was paid, and since much of the material was time-sensitive, the authors paid up. Hollins knew that they could rely on Dad to do the work promptly. The letter that sent Dad into a rage was from Hollins.

"Liz, I was pissed off at their saying I was unreliable because they couldn't get hold of me instantly when they wanted me."

"They have a point with the last part of that complaint, Phil. They can only get in touch with you once a week, and never in person."

"I told them that when I decided to move out here, and they said they were okay with it."

"But that was two years ago. Things have changed with this recession. They are probably feeling the pinch like we are. They're probably downsizing. Lots of companies are. And that means they tot up the good points and the not-so-good points of everyone they do business with, and the fact that you're not readily available becomes a mark against you."

"Whose side are you on, anyway? A wife is supposed to support her husband."

"I'm supporting you in that I want you to think seriously about how you can respond to this setback."

"Then tell me how I'm supposed to make a living when my job has blown up in my face."

"You might get another job."

"Where? Do you think I should go to work at that mill like Steve?"

"I'm sure there are jobs you can do in Caribou."

"And leave this place; my life's dream?"

"If we have to in order to survive."

Listening to them, my reaction was," Yeah, Mom! Way to go."

But Dad's reaction was the complete opposite. "No way am I going to leave this place and go back to live in some city."

"Well then," Mom said calmly, "figure out how you're going to keep your career going without the help of Hollins."

"And how am I supposed to do that?"

"Advertise. That's how you started your editing business."

There was a pause, and I could imagine Dad pacing the floor. "Okay," he said finally. "I can do that."

"You have all the names and addresses of people you've done work for. Send them a letter offering them your services, without the intermediary of Hollins. Be careful how you word it, and for heaven's sake, don't say anything negative about Hollins. You don't want them suing you. Send a letter to other publishers as well."

"Okay, okay, I'll do that."

Good. Now let's go to bed and get some sleep."

Chapter Thirty-Two

One afternoon, Stone dropped by to talk to Dad, saying that he had to go to a meeting of Caribou high school teachers and wouldn't be back for two or three days. If only I'd waited to raid his workshop! I'd only gotten out by the skin of my teeth that day when he had been absent about an hour. If I'd waited I would have had at least two days. Oh well. I supposed professional burglars also run into those situations, where their victims returned home sooner than expected, or where access would have been easy if they had only known something ahead of time.

Old Stoneface had plenty of time to buy himself a new padlock while he was in Caribou, so one day after he returned, I rode past his house and turned down toward the creek, passing along the fence on the side of his property where the workshop was located. I felt a bit nervous about doing this, especially when he strode out of his house and stared at me until I had passed his property and was riding along the creek. I did notice, however, as I rode past the workshop, that there was a new combination lock on the door, this time hanging down normally from the hasp, not cocked up at an angle. I considered for an instant that I might stop and ask for our padlock, but thought better of it. I also wanted to thumb my nose at him, but he never took his eyes off me, so I decided I'd better not.

In the days that followed, he did not return our padlock, even though he stopped by to talk to Dad a couple of times. Around here, neighbours often borrowed from each other, but they always returned the borrowed property. In a small community like this, people have to work together. You help your neighbour when he needs it, and you know that you can call on him when you need help. Both the Hermans and the Monkes had helped us with our construction projects, as had Steve Carlssen. But Stoneface didn't fit in. It suited me however. I still had the key, and if he ever used the padlock on some other place that I might like to get into, I'd have the means to do it. I was feeling a bit cocky about having succeeded in my first break and enter adventure.

The next time Dad went to town, he was still grumpy when he came back. Penny and I didn't pay much attention to him, though, because our new curriculum and new lessons arrived in the mail and we poured over them with interest.

Getting those lessons reminded me that next year, I would be starting high school. If Mom and Dad decided to go to Caribou where Dad could get a job, I would be going to Caribou High next year. But Dad squelched the idea of getting a job in the city, so things remained the same.

I hoped my folks would agree to send me to some real school. They wouldn't send me to live with paternal grandparents in the States. They liked the school system in Canada better than the one in Idaho. My maternal grandparents lived in a suburb of Calgary, and maybe I could I go there to live with them. Or was there some way for me to go to Caribou? The high school kids from Arrow boarded with families in Benson's Bridge, the next town down the river beyond Arrow, where there was a small high school. Junior hockey players, most of whom were high school age, were billeted with families in the towns where they played, going to school in that town.

Maybe I could start working on Mom and Dad gradually over the winter to get them into the right frame of mind so I could ask. It wasn't until several years later that I learned that my folks were worrying about the same thing;

where they could send me for high school. They had come up with the same ideas of how that might be done as the ones I had. I wish they had told me back then about their deliberations. I would have felt a lot better that winter.

Chapter Thirty-Three

The weather cleared and the sun returned. The meadow had a freshly scrubbed look and smelled of all the natural perfumes from wildflowers, and other plants. This would be a good time, I decided, to explore the terrain to the east, over toward the mountains that overlooked the town of Arrow. As soon as we finish our chores, Penny and I saddled our horses and headed off in that direction. As we passed the Herman house, we saw Grace out in her garden and stopped to chat.

"We sure did need that rain," she said, "but it made these weeds grow like mad." She straightened up and rubbed her back. "I've been pulling them for over an hour, and I think they grow back as quick as I pull them up. If you kids stop here on your way back, I'll send a bunch of carrots and beets home with you, and I'll see what else is producing." We promised to stop on our way home.

Before the road turned upward and to the south-east to follow the creek toward the place the fake miners had grown their pot, a primitive road, which was not much more than a couple of wheel tracks over the uneven ground, continued on eastward. It crossed the creek on a bridge made by laying two large tree trunks across the creek, placing two-by-sixes across them at intervals, and laying large boards along the top at the width to just match the wheels of a light vehicle. The bridge wasn't wide enough for trucks, and it looked to have been built fairly recently. It was in good condition. I assumed that Con Monke, who had his base camp for hunting expeditions out here somewhere, had built the bridge. The horses shied at the bridge, so we rode down to the side of the creek where we found a shallow spot where horses obviously crossed. Our horses seemed to know this trail.

On the other side of the creek, the land rose gently toward distant, heavily forested hills. The trees formed a tunnel. Their scent permeated the air in the coolness of the shade. After a while, the road emerged out into the open, the hillside gently forested. Looking back, we could no longer see the meadow, but were following a dry canyon. The ground became rocky. We passed an old logging road leading up toward the south. Beyond this we came upon an old clear-cut, one that had been harvested before the modern practice of cleaning up and re-foresting. It left a messy scar on the hillside. We quickly rode on, Penny scowling and commenting acidly about the ugliness the loggers had left.

"Maybe we could get a job up here to plant some new trees," she suggested.

"I wonder who owns it. We'd have to get permission," I replied.

"Oh well. Let's get out of sight of it." She urged her horse into a ground-covering trot until we could no longer see the clear-cut.

We rode on for another half hour. Knowing that our home was about three miles from the cliff overlooking Arrow, I thought we ought to be getting near the cliff.

A bend in the track brought us out into a level meadow, and in it we saw a fenced pasture with three horses grazing. One of them was Con Monke's pinto packhorse.

So this must be Con's base camp where hunters came in the fall. As we rode into the meadow, we could see where tents had been erected, and privies built. There were no structures at this time, except for one shed which was probably where Con stored supplies, but since Con was apparently bringing in some horses, he would probably soon be setting up his camp for the fall hunting season.

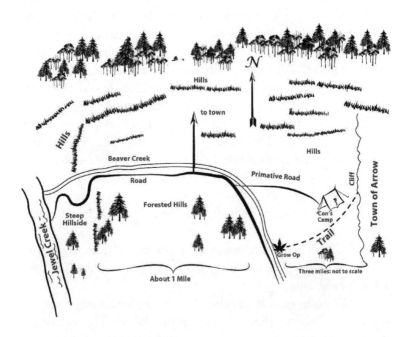

As we rode into the meadow, my horse whinnied a greeting to the horses in the pasture. They raised their heads, answered the greeting and came galloping over to the fence. We rode over and the horses renewed their old acquaintance with neighs and grunts, and nuzzled each other's necks.

Penny, the animal lover, jumped off her horse and went to the fence to pat and talk to the pastured horses. I had other plans. We had left rope halters on under the bridles so we could tie up the horses if we wanted to explore on foot.

We tied our horses to fence posts, and while Penny stayed to commune with the horses, I set out to see what was over the next rise.

To the east of the meadow, a steep, rocky slope appeared to buttress a fairly level grassy ledge, and behind that rose a dense clump of trees. I couldn't find a path. It seemed that no one else was interested in seeing what was beyond the trees. I scrambled over rocks, using an outstretched hand to steady myself, and reached the ledge. To the north, the trees were more widely spaced, so I decided to skirt the really dense patch. I could see blue sky through the trees, so I thought I might be able to reach the crest of the cliff overlooking the town. I made my way through the trees on slightly rising ground, and soon found myself looking at the top of the cliff.

To my surprise, a path led to a spot at the edge of the cliff. The path seemed to come up from the forested area to the south, not from the meadow. I followed this path a short distance. It ended at an open spot at the top of the cliff where a log had been used as a barricade to keep anyone from falling off. An upended block of wood provided a seat for someone who wanted to view the scenery below. Somehow, I doubted whether this set-up was meant for idle tourists. There must be a better reason for it to be there. I went to the edge of the cliff, leaned on the log, and peered down at the town of Arrow, spread out before me. I was looking straight down at the vet clinic on the south edge of town, and I could see a moving black speck in the run where the dog, Jet, was exercised. Someone with binoculars would be able to see him plainly.

Wow! I wondered if this was where those fake miners had come to see if the drug-sniffing dog was being used so they could tell whether it was safe to cross the border with their shipment of pot. Or was this simply a fanciful idea I had conjured up because I wanted to discover how a real crime was worked? Should I follow the obvious path a ways? This lookout must not be far from the site of that grow op, and maybe this trail even led down there. Maybe there was a place at the south end of Con's camp that connected with this trail. If so, I could go back to Penny and the horses that way. Why not? If the trail went off in some other direction, I could always come back up here. Besides, there was no hurry. Penny would be happy with the horses for a while, so I had lots of time to explore this trail.

    The answer was given to me when I turned back the way I had come. There it was! Sticking up out of the clump of trees was the antenna I had been looking for.

Chapter Thirty Four

That antenna had to be mounted some place where the radio was located. Disregarding Sgt. Ross's instruction to get away from the site as quickly as possible, I wove my way between the tightly packed trees until I found the base of the antenna. There was nothing there, but a wire led on down through the trees, strung about six feet off the ground from tree to tree. I followed the wire, through the dense forest, never letting it out of my sight.

I eventually emerged into a small clearing among the trees where a small cabin—really more like a shed—was hidden. It was substantially built and was covered with a sod roof where grass and weeds, and one enormous thistle, grew. There were no windows and the heavy plank door was secured with a heavy-duty padlock that put the one we had loaned to Old Stoneface to shame. The place was a fortress. It was also made to be invisible from the air.

My anxiety at disobeying Sgt. Ross' advice had been increasing as I searched through the woods, and it now broke out in earnest. The sweat on my face was not entirely from the heat. In fact, it was actually pretty cool up there. My stomach cramped and my breathing got faster. I've got to get out of here, I thought. Right now.

I zigzagged through more trees, always going downhill, always looking for a tree that was in a direct line from the ones I had left, and keeping it in sight until I reached it. Finally I broke out of the trees onto the grassy ledge. I found a place where I could slip and slide down the rocky bank, losing some skin on the way, but not caring, I wanted to run toward the horses, but I had to slow down and not look as scared as I was, so I wouldn't frighten Penny or startle the horses. When I got close, I slowed down, pulled myself together and tried to act nonchalant as I walked up to Penny who was still communing with the horses.

"C'mon. Let's go."

I don't know whether she sensed my anxiety or was merely tiring of the horses, but she agreed readily. We swung into our saddles and headed back down the road. I set a fast pace but Penny pulled up beside me.

"Hey, brud, what's going on? Why are you in such a hurry?"

"Chad told me a couple of times that Con didn't like people hanging around his base camp, so I thought it was time for us to leave."

"But he wasn't there, so what's the hurry?"

"I don't want to meet him on the road if he comes up here."

"So what? It's Crown land and it's open to the public. He doesn't have a special claim on it."

"Yes he does. He has a permit for his camp up there."

"Oh, you're making an issue of something that anybody might do. He can't throw us off," she grumbled, but she nevertheless kept up with my rapid pace.

I couldn't tell Penny the real reason I wanted to get out of there. It might scare her, and she might tell someone else, and that could put us in danger if the wrong person found out that we knew the location of that secret radio.

We were riding by the clear-cut and nearing the old logging road I had noticed on the way up when I heard Con Monke's Jeep coming up the road. I could tell the sound of that Jeep anywhere. I kicked my horse into a gallop, looking over my shoulder to make sure Penny was following. She was. I turned up the logging road and slowed Blaze to a walk just as Con's Jeep rounded a corner and came into view. Penny was right beside me. Con stopped at the base of the logging road and I turned in the saddle and gave him a friendly wave.

"What are you kids doing?" he called out.

I reined Blaze around and responded in a cheerful voice, "We thought we'd explore this old road. We've never been up this way before."

"It don't go nowhere, only over to the border. It's all clear-cut up there. There's nothing worth seeing." His tone of voice was not friendly. To my imagination, it sounded threatening.

"Oh," I said, trying to sound disappointed. I'd suddenly realized that there might be more to the story I told Penny. After all, Con's camp was right there below that locked shed with its antenna. Was he the one who used the radio?

Penny piped up, "Well, if there's nothing up there, we might as well go back." She dug her heels into her horse's sides. Peanuts didn't want to go; she was no leader, and was used to following Blaze. I pulled up alongside her, waving to Con as we turned down the road toward home. As we passed Con's Jeep, I saw a revolver in its holster on the seat beside him. Once we were on the road back down to the valley, I heard the Jeep start on up the hill and let out my breath.

"He didn't need to be so nasty," Penny complained.

"Yeah."

"Okay brud. Give. What's going on? It isn't just because he doesn't like people to mess with his campsite."

Should I, or shouldn't I, tell Penny the real story?

"Can you keep a secret? It's important," I said.

"Sure. Cross my heart." She made a crossing motion.

"All right. It's dangerous, though, so you can't ever tell anyone. I'm serious. I really mean it."

"I said I wouldn't tell, and I won't. I know you're up to something, and I don't want to be left in the dark."

"Okay. Remember when Sgt. Ross asked me to watch for a radio antenna?"

"Yeah."

"Well, I found it."

Her eyes nearly popped out. "Where?"

"Up there in those woods above Con's camp. I saw the antenna sticking up out of the trees and followed the wire that ran from it to a shed hidden in the woods. The shed's locked up, tighter than a drum. Remember Sgt. Ross telling me to get away from the area if I found an antenna?"

"I don't remember that, but I suppose he did."

"Well, that's why I want to get as far away from there as I can."

"If that radio is up there where Con's camp is, it must be his."

"I don't think so. There's no trail up to those trees from his camp. There is a trail that goes off to the south. Con probably doesn't even know that shed is there. There wouldn't be any reason for him ever to go up there."

I tried to sound sure of myself, but I had my doubts when I'd seen Con coming, and to be safe, I wanted to get out of his way. Reason told me that what I said to Penny was probably the truth. Still, Con would know we'd been up there. We must have left tracks galore. He wouldn't have to be an expert tracker to figure out that the tracks of two shod horses were those of our horses, left when we'd been up there. I shuddered at the thought that I might have brought my little sister into mortal danger when I let her come with me.

Chapter Thirty-Five

As we rode on, I kept thinking about the possibilities. Those guys who were growing the pot had cleaned out their cabin and scrammed out of there in a big hurry after burying the body. I wondered if they had removed the radio also, but didn't have time to take down the antenna. That shed might be empty. But then why lock it?

And then there was the man I'd seen walking down the far hillside when the cops were digging up the grave. Could he have gone up there to that shed to get the radio? Because I had only been able to see his legs, I hadn't been able to see whether he was carrying anything. Was he the local conspirator the police thought must exist? But it couldn't have been Con, I reasoned, because Con would have been on horseback.

I was still turning these thoughts over in my mind when we reached the bottom of the hill. We took the trail around the bridge, the horses stopping to drink from the creek. At the Herman place, we rode in and tied our horses to the fence around the front yard of the house. Grace came to the door to greet us.

"I've made some lemonade," she said. "Come on in." It was hot down here in the valley, and the cool drink tasted wonderful.

"I hope you don't mind us always stopping by here," Penny said, politely.

"Not at all, honey. I enjoy having kids around. When mine all fled the nest, I was pretty lonely. Erma Monke was lonely too, so we would exchange visits. She's a really good cook and I have all this garden stuff, so we would always make an excuse to get together. Then when her kids got old enough, they would come over here, so I had young ones around me again.

"When Conner, who was a nice boy, left for high school, he went to work with his father during summer vacations, so I didn't see much of him any more. Darlene came back out here her first summer after she started high school. She hated living out here and wanted school to start again so she could go back to town. The next summer, she just stayed in town and lived with her boyfriend's parents. I don't like to be judgemental, but I don't think it was a good idea. She got pregnant and had her first baby when she was barely sixteen. She had to be sixteen before she could marry the boy. She has another child, and I think she's pregnant again. I hope the marriage lasts, or she'll have a hard time raising three kids on her own. The boy works at a mill where his dad works, and he makes good money. I don't know whether he's old enough to work there legally, but his boss doesn't seem to care."

"Was there an elementary school here in the valley in those days?" I asked.

"No, there never was. The kids all went to school in Arrow, and Monke drove them over the divide to where they could catch the school bus every day. We did the same with ours when they were little."

My folks could have done that for me, I thought bitterly. I didn't have to be stuck out here in the boonies all the time. I didn't say anything though.

Grace went on, "That younger boy, Chad, never did come over here, so I hardly know him. All he wanted to do was hang out with his big brother. I know he goes riding with you, Derek, but I haven't seen him much this summer."

"I haven't either," I mumbled. The less said about Chad, the better I liked it.

"Kids do grow up kind of quick out here in this country. I expect he has other interests nowadays."

Fortunately, Grace then changed the subject. "Were did you go on your ride?"

"We went up to Con's base camp. Some of his horses are there, and they recognized ours and had a reunion." Penny explained, laughing.

Grace frowned. "I'd be careful riding up there. Conner doesn't like people going anywhere near his camp when he's not there. He pointed a rifle at some guys he caught up there once. They were looking for stuff to steal. He didn't shoot anyone, and he said the gun wasn't loaded, but he sure had fun telling about seeing those guys run for their lives."

"Yeah. We met him on our way back. All he told us was that there weren't any good places to ride up that way because it's all clear-cut." I held my breath, hoping that Penny wouldn't say any more. She didn't.

I changed the subject of discussion. "It doesn't seem like a good place for a hunting camp. It's in that corner between the cliff and the border fence, and if it's all clear-cut around there, where do they go hunting?"

"Oh, that makes it good hunting," Grace replied. "There is lots of brush growing up in those clear-cuts, and that makes good browse for the deer. But the main reason is that Conner is young, and all the better spots had been taken by other outfitters who'd been doing it for years."

"Well, it's a nice spot for a camp, with that big meadow for pasture for his horses. Have you been up there?"

"No, I haven't. But I'm glad to hear that it's a nice spot. I hope Conner succeeds as an outfitter and guide. He needs something to do other than just working for his dad."

"Where does this road go when it heads up into the hills? I don't know of anyone else who lives up that way, but it's a good gravel road."

"It's an access road to the border fence for when they go up there to inspect it or do maintenance. You can go for miles along the fence. That's another reason Conner's camp isn't in such a bad place. His hunters can go along the fence and look down into the timber. There are also a couple of places where people can camp. They're kind of out-of-the-way, and don't have water, so they aren't used much."

"Where does the creek come from? We've never been up that way very far."

"From a little lake up there in the mountains on the American side of the border, I've heard. The road doesn't follow it all the way up."

We spent a pleasant hour chatting, and when we left, Grace gave us bags of veggies from her garden, one for each of us so we could hang them on our saddle horns. "There was still some corn, so I put some ears in there," Grace said. "The squash are getting near being ready to harvest, so I'll send Bill over with some when they're ready. He's down at your place right now. He and Phil are talking about building a better barn for your horses and cow. Bill's always needed to be busy, and since we don't farm any more, he loves helping your dad."

I waited until Dad and Bill were finished discussing the new structure and Bill left. Then I cornered Dad before he got busy with something else.

"Dad, I have something I need to tell you."

"Don't bother me now, son. I'm busy."

"It's important, Dad."

"Okay. But be quick about it."

"Remember when Sgt. Ross was here talking to us, he asked me to watch out for an antenna when I was out riding. They want to find someone with a CB radio."

"I don't approve of the cops using kids to snoop for them. They should do their own work."

"But they're always asking citizens for help. They can't be everywhere"

"Well, I'm not a citizen of Canada, and I don't like it."

"Dad, listen. I found the antenna. He told me that if I did, I should tell you so you can call them next time you're in town."

"Is there a law in this country about someone having a radio?"

"But this was hidden out in the woods, and there was a shed hidden in the trees that must be where the radio is. Dad, you've got to tell them. I can show them where it is."

"I'm not going to go out of my way to call them."

"Dad, I promised. If they find out I know where the radio is and didn't tell them, Sgt. Ross will be mad at me."

"Okay, okay. I'll call them the next time I go to town."

But as it turned out, he didn't.

Chapter Thirty-Six

Dad was still in a grouchy mood the next morning, and it didn't improve when, about seven o'clock in the morning, two police vehicles drove by and stopped in front of Old Stoneface's cabin.

"What are they doing at Stone's?" Dad growled. "I'm going down and find out." He strode purposefully down the road.

Penny and I both felt a sense of excitement, knowing that something momentous was about to happen, so we scrambled over the rocky outcroppings between our place and Stoneface's. At the top of the last one, we lay down on our bellies to watch the action. Dad had already reached the cabin and seemed to be calling to someone inside. Soon a policeman appeared at the door. We couldn't hear what they were talking about, but with each exchange of words, Dad appeared to become angrier. The cop tried to shoo him away, but he stood his ground. We could hear him shouting, although we couldn't hear what he was saying. He gesticulated wildly. The cop grabbed him by the arm, turned him around and escorted him to the gate, pushed him through it, and slammed the gate shut. He said something to Dad, and made a gesture that reminded me of the time we had tried to shoo the friendlier of the Monkes' two dogs away from our house. Dad retreated a short distance, then stood his ground. The cop went back into the cabin.

We continued our vigil. The policemen went to the workshop and opened the lock. They must have gotten the combination from Old Stoneface. They were in there for some time and eventually came out carrying a box, which we assumed contained items they were confiscating. Dad renewed his assault, opening the gate and marching around to the shop. Again he was forcefully escorted back out to the road. The cop's actions were firm, and I could imagine him telling Dad, in no uncertain terms, to get out of their way and let them do their work.

The police stowed the box they had removed from the workshop in one of their vehicles. A few minutes later they led Old Stoneface out to the other car. He was handcuffed.

"Wow! Look at that. They're arresting him. I wonder what he did," Penny exclaimed.

"Yeah, and look at Dad. They're going to arrest Dad, too, if he doesn't shut up." Two cops advanced toward Dad. I could tell that they meant business, and that business was to get Dad out of their hair. He finally got the point and headed back along the road toward our place. He didn't go willingly, and kept stopping to look behind him at what was happening at Stoneface's cabin. Penny and I raced home, excited as kids always are at the sight of police at work. We saw the car carrying Old Stoneface go by, while the other car remained at the cabin.

Dad's face was bright red, his hands were clenched into fists, and his breathing was heavy when he got back home. He raged for a good ten minutes about the action of the police.

"Stone is a decent guy," he shouted. "I don't know what they think they're doing, taking him away in handcuffs. I don't know what this country is coming to if they can just walk into someone's house and drag him out like that."

No one bothered to remind Dad that the police must have some evidence that Old Stoneface had committed a crime that was serious enough to warrant his arrest. Mom turned her back and went on with her work in the kitchen.

Penny and I scrambled up to our loft and conversed in low tones. All of us wanted to stay out of Dad's way.

We listened avidly to the news broadcast that evening, but there was nothing about the arrest. Dad was planning to go into Arrow the next day anyway, so he would undoubtedly bring back news.

"I'll get to the bottom of this," he vowed.

Sure enough, Dad brought back a newspaper along with the local scuttlebutt about Stone's arrest. It was on the news that evening as well. Stone had been charged with sending letter bombs to a total of four people. Those named were the first four on that list I'd seen in the workshop. Nothing was said about the fifth person on that list. Presumably the police had seen the list in Stone's workshop, and would notify the fifth person and tell him to watch his mail and not to open any padded mailers or large manila envelopes (which the first three bombs had been sent in) and to notify the police if any such envelopes arrived.

The four recipients of these exploding missives had been men who were prominent in the oil industry in one way or another. One was the CEO of a pipeline company. Another was a chemical engineer who was working on more efficient methods of transporting oil. The third was a top-level employee of a company involved in extracting oil from the northern Alberta oil sands. The letter bomb I had seen in the workshop was destined for a member of parliament who was promoting pipelines as being a better way to ship oil than by railcar. I might agree with Dad's disapproval of rampant oil production and increasing use, but that was not an excuse for killing people involved in the oil business.

The first letter had been opened by the man's secretary. The blast had resulted in serious, and permanent, damage to her right hand as well as disfiguring scars on her face. The second had killed the man to whom it was sent, who opened it himself. The third recipient had suspected a bomb and notified the police. The last bomb that Old Stoneface sent had been intercepted by police before it could be delivered.

Stone had been on the RCMP's list of possible suspects because of his rabid denunciation of the oil industry. He had been a chemistry professor at an Alberta university, and had been fired, he claimed, because the university got large grants from the oil industry and didn't want to be associated with protests against those businesses. He could not get a position with any other university, and had ended up teaching high school science.

Based on what the police found in the two intact packages they had confiscated, one from the workshop and the other from the third victim, they could trace the source of the explosive and the detonators back to their source, and that had confirmed to them that Stone was their prime suspect.

I devoured everything I could, written or broadcast, about the case. I wished we could get better radio or TV reception. There had obviously been a learning curve involved in the packaging of the bombs. The first bomb had not been powerful enough to kill, only to maim. The second produced a bigger blast. It had been in an envelope with the prominent label saying 'Personal' so it would not be opened by a secretary. The third recipient had recognized the large manila envelope with something solid inside as a possible bomb, so Stone had changed the packaging for the fourth bomb. Perhaps the fifth would have been in a small box.

The packages were mailed from a different city each time: Red Deer and Lethbridge in Alberta, Chilliwack and Vernon in BC, so it was impossible to pin down the location of the person who sent them. I remembered that each time a bomb was reported, Stone had either just arrived in the valley, or had gone away for several days, presumably to get to a distant city to mail his weapon.

I had a hard time resisting the desire to crow about having known the contents of that last package. I'd seen the bomb in the process of being built, and when I'd read those names in the paper I removed from my ceiling, I'd known what Old Stoneface's 'business' was. Nevertheless, I think I succeeded in looking as surprised as everyone else when he was arrested. The arrest was a bit of excitement in an otherwise boring time.

It soon became obvious that Dad had forgotten to, or maybe had found an excuse not to, call the RCMP about the antenna I had located. No one came out to investigate. No one tried to get in touch with us. I found this a bit weird, since Sgt. Ross had been so anxious to find it. Should I remind Dad again? He had been in such a foul mood recently (and an even more foul one now that his friend, Stone, had been arrested) that I hesitated to ask him whether he had made the call. So I let it slide, thinking the police would probably come out to ask again some time. But as the weeks went by, nothing happened. No one showed up. Other things were occupying the Mounties minds, I guessed.

One day, about a month after I had found the antenna, Dad took me to town with him. But I thought it was too late to call now about something that happened a month ago. I didn't think they would pay as much attention to me as they would to Dad if he called anyway. So I didn't do anything.

I got the mail from our post office box while Dad picked up the faxes waiting for him. I handed him several letters, which he riffled through and then sat down to read. A couple of them seemed to delight him. When I went over to sit beside him, I saw why. He pulled cheques out of two of the envelopes, and when I saw the amounts on them, I knew that our financial troubles were over, at least for the time being. It seemed that his advertising and letter-writing campaigns had paid off.

Dad's demeanour changed dramatically. When we went to the café for lunch, he even let me order a double bacon cheeseburger with fries, something Mom would never have let me eat.

I hadn't realized how precarious our finances had been. Life got better around home after that.

Chapter Thirty-Seven

After a pleasant Indian summer, the rains came, driving us indoors to our lessons and books. We had done so well with our lessons the previous year that the school sent us extra, non-required, projects to do. I got some high-school level course material. They were much more of a challenge than our regular lessons, and Penny and I loved the new stuff. We had always done well in school, and we enjoyed the extra mental demands the more advanced courses required.

This area of the province had a regional library, with a small branch in Arrow. If we ran out of interesting books to read, we could order others, which would be delivered the next time the library book truck came to town. I liked science books and biographies, or autobiographies, of successful people. In the fiction line, I went for mysteries and westerns. I didn't care for sci-fi. Science fact was much more interesting. It was a good thing that we had access to library books, because I found the assigned reading for my English Lit. course rather boring. I loved to read, often staying up late into the night.

Penny and I went riding whenever the weather was good enough, but with so much rain, the horses were getting a lot of rest after all the work they did over the summer. They began to get fat.

In January, winter hit with a vengeance. The temperature at night dropped to minus thirty degrees Celsius. Penny figured that out to be about twenty-six degrees below zero Fahrenheit. Penny was supposed to be so good with numbers, but then I found out that she had merely looked at the thermometer outside our kitchen window, which showed both scales. It was slightly frosted over so it was hard to read accurately, so I still didn't know whether she was correct. So much for her vaunted mathematical skills. Anyway, it was cold!

We had a hard time keeping the house warm with only the kitchen stove for heat. When we lived in the tent, it had been a rule that anyone who got up during the night had to put some wood on the fire in the stove. If no one did, the fire would go out and we'd have to rebuild the fire and wait impatiently for our home to warm up in the morning. We still had this rule even here in the house. It could get awfully cold if the fire went out, but at least water didn't freeze, as it would have done in the tent. Penny had the side of the loft that had a finished ceiling, so it was slightly warmer than my side, but I had the stovepipe coming up through my room. I could sit near it, or hang clothes to dry on a line I strung across the room, near the stovepipe.

Speaking of hanging out clothes, in winter we had clothes racks all over the place when it was cold or snowing or raining, which was most of the time. In the summer, we hung our clothes out on an outdoor line. Mom said later that the thing she remembered most about winter on Beaver Creek was the smell of wet wool clothes drying in the kitchen.

We found an old washing machine, complete with wringer, in an antique shop in a town across the border in Washington (the state, that is). It was run with a gasoline motor. It was very hard to start, requiring a very firm pull on the lanyard attached to the motor. It usually took several tries before it would agree to start. Mom trying to start the washing machine was the only time I ever heard her swear.

Grace Herman said she used to use a washer of that type, and we should be very careful in using the wringer, because if you get your fingers caught in the wringer while feeding the clothes into it, she told us, it can mangle them. Wringers of this type are appropriately called mangles. There is a release lever to get the rollers to part if you do get your hand caught, but by that time, the mangle has done its worst to your hand.

We learned that we should get clothes that didn't need ironing, or else wear them in spite of the wrinkles. Dad still liked his shirts ironed, but Mom hated having to use a flatiron heated on the stove. She had trouble figuring out when the iron was hot enough, and often scorched something she was ironing. She scorched one of Dad's dress shirts and he got mad.

"Why don't you watch what you're doing," he yelled.

Mom slammed the iron back on the stove and snarled, "If you don't like it, you can just do it yourself."

"Don't talk to me like that."

"Don't *you* talk to *me* like that, either. I've had enough of this. I'm going for a walk." She walked out the door and didn't come back for more than an hour.

No-iron shirts were a good idea.

Chapter Thirty-Eight

Bill Herman arrived at our house on a cold day in early March. He looked worried.

"Liz, can you come and help me out? Grace is real sick, and I need to do the cooking and I'm not any good at it." We had noticed over the last week or two that Grace was coughing a lot, although that wasn't unusual, considering the long cold spell.

Mom gathered up some cans of soup and a few other food items, put them in a bag, put on her boots and warm coat, and went with Bill in his truck. Soon after, Bill came back, saying that Mom planned to stay at the Herman house for a few days, and wanted Penny to come and help her.

Dad and I stayed home. We could take care of ourselves. Dad could do some basic cooking, and Mom had taught both Penny and me to cook balanced meals, thinking that both of us would be on our own some day and would need to feed ourselves properly. Dad and I conjured up some good stews, using whatever was handy or attracted our fancy at the moment.

This father/son sharing turned out to be a boon to both of us. I had begun to feel alienated from Dad, and this sharing of household duties brought us back together. There was a difference this time. I was now fifteen, and Dad was beginning to treat me like a man, not like a boy. I felt that we'd passed a turning point in my life. From now on, I would be expected to act like an adult, and was given more responsibility for my actions. Dad let me drive the pickup out here on this rural road where no one would stop me and ask to see my licence. I had watched his driving intently all my life and felt very comfortable sliding into the driver's seat, though it would be another year before I could start the graduated licencing course of learner and novice required of the province before I could get a full license.

"Derek, you've gotten a lot more mature over the last two years. I'm proud of you."

"Thanks, Dad." I was pleased that Dad approved of me.

"And you get your school work done without prompting," he went on. "You used to dislike school."

"It wasn't the stuff I had to learn that I didn't like. It was just going to school. I'd get bored because I got stuff done before anyone else, and there was nothing else to do. If I tried to do anything, the teachers would tell me to quit, and if I just sat still and stared off into space, they'd accuse me of being lazy, or not paying attention to what I was supposed to do."

"You seem to concentrate on your schoolwork now. I don't see you goofing off."

"Yeah, I like the assignments, especially these more advanced ones they're sending me now. And when I'm done, I get to do something else."

"See, that's another good thing that has come from moving out here."

Oh, oh, I thought in despair. I really put my foot in it. Quickly, I tried to repair the damage. "But I don't get to hang around with other kids. I never see any kids out here."

"There's Chad."

"Uh, I don't hang out with him much any more."

"Why not?"

"Well, I don't like some of the things he does. When we lived in town, I had lots of friends."

Dad apparently didn't get the message. He seemed to lose interest in the subject. Peering at a Bisquick box, he asked, "What does your mom put in this stuff when she makes pancakes?"

"She uses an egg and milk. Here, let me do it."

"Okay, I'll do the eggs. How do you like yours done?"

But our new relationship was about to receive a severe test.

I went every day to the Hermans' place with a bottle of cream-rich milk from our Jersey cow. Grace, who seldom drank milk, found that she liked the fresh milk, so we took all of it to her. The cow had been bred to one of the Monkes' range bulls with the idea that the calf would be good meat quality for us to use later. Our cow was now drying up, and we were buying milk in large jugs whenever we went to town. We couldn't have done that in the summer because we didn't have any refrigeration. During the winter, however, the problem was not one of keeping the milk cool, but of keeping it from freezing. We gave the small amount of milk our cow was still producing to Grace. The cow was due to calve in late spring and we would then have milk again.

On one of my trips to the Hermans, driving the pickup of course, I sensed a new feeling of anxiety in their household. Grace was becoming weaker every day and had taken to her bed for good. Mom asked her if she would like to be taken out to Caribou, where there was a hospital, but Grace adamantly refused.

"I don't want to be stuck in any hospital. I want to stay here," she insisted.

Mom suggested to Bill that he should try to get her to go. "She will get better much sooner there where they can treat her a lot better than we can here at home. She has pneumonia, you know."

Bill shook his head. "No. For one thing, she won't go. We've talked this over in the past, and both of us agree that we don't want to be hauled off to no hospital if we get sick. We know that we'll both die someday, but we'd rather die in our own bed, not in no hospital."

And that was that; nothing Mom nor Dad said could change Bill's or Grace's mind. We found out later that this was a fairly common attitude of people living in the wilderness in earlier times. When they moved out into the wilderness they reconciled themselves to this view of life and death.

Penny stayed by Grace's side most of the time, nursing her. At first, when Grace could still get up, Penny would help her. She would make Grace's bed, settle her down in it again, prop her up with several pillows (some borrowed from us) because Grace had trouble breathing when lying flat, and hand-feed her liquid or pureed food. She would sit beside Grace, holding her hand and singing the few songs she knew. Penny, Mom, and Bill took turns sitting up with Grace throughout the nights. She developed a deep rumbling chest cough, and her breath was becoming more laboured each day.

When asked, Bill said he realized that his wife of more than fifty years was dying. So did Mom. The one person who did not buy into this idea of life and death was Dad.

"If we can get a helicopter to come out here and pick her up, she'd be in Caribou in no time. If she doesn't want to make the trip in a truck, that would solve the problem. Somebody's got to go out to a phone and call for a medevac helicopter," he insisted.

But Bill merely shook his head. "You don't understand. You city folk always want to call someone for help with every little thing that happens, but you don't understand the pioneer mentality like us who've lived here all our lives do."

Dad was obviously annoyed at being called 'city folk' after spending the last two years pretending to be a frontiersman. He walked away in a huff. But knowing my father, I was sure he wouldn't forget.

Chapter Thirty-Nine

The next day, around mid-morning, we sensed there was a change in the weather. Suddenly water was dripping off the eaves as the snow on the roof began to melt. Then the wind came. I couldn't remember ever having experienced a Chinook, though I knew, from my lessons about weather, that it was a warm wind that blows when moist air has been pushed up a slope, losing its moisture as rain, and the resulting drier air roars down the lea slope, becoming progressively warmer. Soon cascades of water were tumbling down the gullies, filling the streams. The lower end of our pasture flooded, and the water was almost level with the wooden bridge across Beaver Creek.

In the evening, Dad and I drove over to the Hermans' house again, the truck slipping into ruts in the road, which was now a sea of mud. As we walked in, I could feel the change in the atmosphere. Everyone was on edge and wandering around doing little things to take their mind off what was happening in the bedroom. You could have cut the tension with a knife. Dad started to demand an account of how Grace was doing, but Mom shushed him. "Be quiet," she demanded.

"Why? What's up?" he asked in a quieter voice.

"Come into the other room. And keep your voice down."

We trekked into the living room. "Okay, what's the matter?" Dad asked.

"Grace has lost consciousness. We think she's dying. Penny is sitting with her and talking to her, but she doesn't respond."

"Well, that does it," Dad exclaimed in a louder voice. "I'm going out to Arrow and call for a medevac chopper."

Bill hurried into the room upon hearing Dad's outburst. "You can't get to Arrow in this weather," he said.

"Why not?"

"You haven't been here long enough to see what happens to the road when it rains a lot, or when there's a lot of snowmelt running down into the river. The road along the river washes out, and there's rock slides. Nobody with any sense tries to drive into town. They've probably blocked off the road, anyway."

"I've got four-wheel drive and good tires."

"That won't do no good when there's no road to drive on."

"I can't believe it can be that bad after only a few hours of warm weather."

"You'd believe it if you'd lived here longer. Trust me."

I heard a snowmobile come into the yard. The front door opened and Con Monke walked in, carrying a large thermos.

"Mom sent over some soup and said to tell you that she'll come over to help you folks if you need her. And if I can do anything at all for Grace, let me know. She was real good to me when I was a little kid."

"Thanks, Con. That's very kind of you," Bill replied, taking the thermos and carrying it into the kitchen.

"Hey, Phil," Con said. "I heard you talking to Bill about the road. You better pay attention to what he says. He's right. That road over along the river ain't safe to drive on in this type of weather. The water's almost up to the top of our bridge here, and some of the road will probly be under water."

"I don't care," Dad almost shouted. "I'm going to town and I'm going to call for a medevac chopper. No one's going to stop me."

"You're crazy, man. You oughta pay attention."

Mom had heard enough. "Don't be stupid, Phil. Pay attention to what these men say. They know the country."

Dad turned his back, grabbed his coat and shrugged into it.

"Well, I have more guts than they do. Someone has to do something. You can't just sit around here waiting for Grace to die. If nobody else will, I'll do what's right," he shouted over his shoulder as he headed for the door.

"Phil, don't," Mom pleaded, but Dad jerked open the door and strode out into the night. He was back in a few seconds, however.

"Derek, give me the keys." I'd been the one who drove over and I'd put the keys in my pocket. Should I give them to Dad?

"The keys," Dad commanded, holding out his hand. No one else said anything. I hesitantly dug into my pocket, pulled out the keys, and reluctantly handed them over. I stepped out onto the porch and watched him go. He spun the wheels in a jackrabbit start, and I briefly hoped he'd get stuck and not be able to go. But the wheels grabbed, and he roared out of the yard, turned down the road and raced off, slithering on the muddy road. He could be a reckless driver when he got angry and that worried me.

Con followed me out of the house, paused to watch Dad depart, and said to me, "Your Dad's nuts."

He got on his snowmobile and drove away. He didn't turn on his headlight, but I figured he'd do it once he got out of the lighted yard. It was raining hard, and I lost sight of him as soon as he got out of the circle of light from the house. I could hear the snowmobile turn left onto the road, its sound gradually fading away.

Back in the house, the tense vigil continued. Penny was sitting beside Grace's bed talking to her and singing softly, hoping that even though she didn't respond, she still might hear. Bill paced around the room. Mom took a bowl of the soup Con had brought, but when she tried to get Grace to take some, the old woman did not respond. Her breath was becoming increasingly laboured, with an alarming rattle.

Bill moved over to the bedside and said softly to Penny, "Would you mind leaving me alone with her, honey?" Penny got up and left the room, closing the door softly behind her as Bill took her place and held his wife's hand.

"She's dying," Penny told us. We could only nod. We sat down at the kitchen table and waited.

Mom became restless, and a frown appeared on her face.

"I wonder if Bill should be left alone with Grace."

"Of course, he should," Penny exclaimed. "Why shouldn't he?"

"I've been thinking. I wonder if he is the person who the police think collaborated with those men who were growing pot. Maybe Grace knew about it and thought it would help Bill if she told the police she saw Conner come out on the Friday afternoon with that man he had packed in there. We know Conner actually came out late that night and that man wasn't with him. It's only Grace who said Conner came by their place in the afternoon. And for the last few days, he's hasn't done anything to get help for her, and has been giving us that song and dance about Grace wanting to die in her own bed. I wonder if he might just make sure she does."

"Mom! He wouldn't do anything to her. He loves her," Penny admonished.

"He may love her, but he may love himself more, and she is the one who could tell on him."

That aroused me from my dejected muse. "Mom, he didn't kill that man."

"What makes you think so, Derek?"

"I know who did, and it wasn't Bill."

Both Mom and Penny stared at me in disbelief. But before an accounting could be demanded of me, the bedroom door opened and Bill came out, shutting the door behind him."

Penny asked gently, "Is she gone?"

Bill only nodded and wandered out into the living room where he collapsed into his favourite armchair. Penny sat on the arm of the chair, put her arm around his shoulders, leaned her head against his and said simply, "I'm so sorry."

There was no thought of continuing our conversation about the murder.

Chapter Forty

We slept fitfully the rest of the night; Bill in his armchair, Mom on the couch, and Penny and I on other chairs. Early the next morning I borrowed Bill's truck and drove to our place to feed the livestock. The horses and cow were huddled in the shelter of their shed. The lower end of the pasture was flooded, and rivulets of water flowed across the upper portion. I looked at the cow's udder and decided it really wasn't worthwhile milking her any more. Mowser came out of his nest among the hay bales. I gave him a big pan full of cat food, on the assumption that we might not be keeping a regular feeding schedule.

Day was dawning as I drove back to the Hermans'. The wind had dropped to a gentle breeze. The temperature remained warm. A few stars were still winking in the sky between scattered clouds.

Mom was cooking breakfast, although we all said that we were not really hungry. But when the aroma of bacon permeated the house, even Bill came to the table. We were just finishing our breakfast when the sound of a powerful engine, accompanied by the slapping of helicopter blades made us scurry out of the house to see what was happening. The chopper made a beeline for the Herman house and circled low overhead. It was a medevac chopper.

So Dad had gotten out after all!

Bill ran to the large pasture near the house and signalled to the chopper that they should land at the upper end of it where the ground, now free of snow, was the most firm. The chopper circled again, turning into the wind and settling gently at the spot Bill had indicated. Two paramedics climbed out, with a bag of supplies, and ducking to stay clear of the chopper's blades hurried toward the house. Bill met them.

"You're too late," he said. "Grace passed away last night. But thanks for coming."

"We started out as soon as the weather cleared this morning. I'm sorry to hear your news, but let us take a look. They trudged up to the house and went into the bedroom. A few minutes later, they came out.

"We can take her body out to the hospital in Caribou, but we won't be able to take you with us, Mr. Herman. We're sorry, but our chopper is not configured to take an extra person. But the police chopper will be out shortly. They can take you out with them." Bill nodded.

I was pretty sure that what the paramedics meant was that they would take her to the morgue, which was probably at the hospital. But Penny whispered to me, "Maybe she isn't dead after all."

"She is," I told her, "but they're trying not to use words that sound horrible like 'morgue' does."

"Oh." She made a face.

As the paramedics rolled the stretcher carrying Grace's body out of the bedroom, Bill asked urgently, "Don't cover her face!" The paramedics agreed and gently turned down the sheet. Grace's face was relaxed, and I thought, serene. She had lived and died the way she wanted, and had not been anxious about her approaching death. Dad's protest, though well-meant, had been in vain.

One of the pilots exited the chopper and walked over. Speaking to Mom, he asked, "Are you Mrs. Taylor?"

"Yes."

"We have a message from the police for you."

Mom gasped. "W-w-what?"

"They said to tell you that as soon as they can get into the air, and they'll go back along the road to see if they can spot Mr. Taylor's truck. They'll find him."

"Didn't he get to Arrow?"

"No, ma'am. The road's washed out. They were hoping he turned around and came back here, but they're going to look anyway. I gather that he didn't come back." He had obviously noticed the absence of another man and of our silver pickup.

I had a question. "But if he didn't get through, how did you know to come out here this morning?"

"All I know is that some guy who listens to citizens band radio said someone up here had sent a distress call and he was passing the message along."

So that was why the police were coming out in their chopper. I'd wondered about that. The serious illness of a local resident wouldn't have aroused their interest. Maybe Dad hadn't remembered to call to tell them that I'd found out where that radio was, and now they were coming again to look for it, knowing that the radio was still here and was being used. I'd told Mom and Penny the night before that I knew who had murdered that undercover cop. I'd had an inkling for several days that I knew the answer. Now I realized that the last piece of the puzzle had dropped into place. Now I was sure.

The police helicopter showed up around noon. They landed in the same spot the medevac chopper had used. We had stayed at Bill's house to support him until they came.

A Mountie got out and came over to meet us.

"Mrs. Taylor?" he inquired, looking at Mom.

"Yes," she responded anxiously.

"We found your husband. He's alive, but injured. He's been taken to hospital in Caribou. We can give you a lift, so you can visit him. The road will be closed for several days until the water recedes and the highway crews can repair it."

"What happened?"

"He apparently tried to drive through the area along the river where the bank was washing away, and there were slides in that area also. We think a rock may have fallen and hit the rear end of his truck and pushed it around so the rear wheels were on the unstable bank and the truck slid off backward into the river. Or else he might have been trying to turn around. We aren't really sure what happened, because we haven't been able to talk to him yet."

"How badly is he hurt?"

"Pretty bad, I think. The local search and rescue group was lifted out there by their chopper and found him alive, but they couldn't get him out without equipment from the fire department to cut off the top of the truck's cab, so the equipment was brought out by chopper along with a couple of firemen. They pretty much had to dismantle the cab, and to get a backboard under him, they had to take out the back of the seat. His seat belt wasn't fastened, so maybe he had tried to get out, but both doors were jammed, probably because more rocks rolled down on the truck, so there was a lot of damage. Everyone had to be brought in and taken out by chopper. It couldn't land, so they had to use their sling. They got the backboard onto a stretcher, hoisted it out, and took it to where the ambulance was waiting. That SAR group does good work. They sure help us a lot."

I thought back to the time when Dad had stormed out of the Herman house. He'd run out to the truck and jumped in, started it up and roared off like at bat out of hell. He hadn't stopped to fasten his seatbelt. I didn't mention this to the cops. Let them think he had been a good citizen, had fastened his seat belt, and had desperately tried to get out of his damaged truck. I wondered if not wearing the seat belt made a difference in the injuries he got.

"Oh, dear. I'll have to go, but what about the kids?" Mom asked.

"We can take them too, along with Mr. Herman."

"But who'll take care of our animals?"

Steve Carlssen turned up while we were talking. In response to her question, he told her, "Don't worry. I'll take care of them for you. I'll be sure everything is all right at your place."

"How come you're here?" Mom asked

"I heard all these choppers coming and going and was wondering what was going on, so I thought I'd better come over and see if you guys needed any help."

"Thanks Steve." Mom gave him a hug.

The Mountie advised, "Get some things together that you'll need for a few days and we'll get going."

Steve drove us to our house where we quickly changed, threw some clothes into our backpacks, and went back to the waiting chopper.

Chapter Forty-One

The flight out was the first time any of us had ridden in a helicopter. Mom was a bit nervous, but Penny and I were excited. As we rose above the scattered clouds, I could see the layout of the valley and realized that what had seemed huge while riding over it on horseback, wasn't that big after all when seen all of a piece. The whole place still looked as if covered with water, with pools and small streams converging toward the swollen creek, and the wet look of the rest of the land. We didn't fly over the site of Dad's wreck, and I realized that the pilot must have deliberately not flown a direct course to Caribou when, after crossing the river, he changed course again.

They had called ahead to give our ETA, which the pilot told me meant 'estimated time of arrival.' At the hospital, people were waiting for us. One of them took charge of Bill. We said a hasty goodbye to him, and that was the last time any of us ever saw our nice helpful neighbour. Our escort took us into the ER, where the receptionist greeted us and said she would inform the team working with Dad that his family had arrived. A nurse appeared to escort Mom to his bedside.

"He isn't conscious," she warned Mom, "but you can stay with him a while. She then had an afterthought. "Are you two his children?"

We nodded.

"Okay, you can come, too."

I wondered later if she had let us come because Dad was still in critical condition and this might be our only opportunity to see him alive. We didn't stay long because we were obviously in the way. The doctor in charge of his care explained Dad's injuries and treatment.

"We are trying to get his body temperature up. He was seriously hypothermic. That's why he is all wrapped up. We only stopped long enough to get a CT scan, since it was obvious that he had a spinal injury. His spine is fractured, but the good news is that his spinal cord, though badly damaged, is not severed. He also has a fractured femur and other lesser injuries. He will require surgery, but it will be done at Royal Valley Hospital in Fairview, not here. Once we have him stabilized, and his body temperature out of the danger range, he will be airlifted up there. In the meantime, we have sedated him to keep him from injuring himself further. He was in and out of consciousness, and when he would wake, he kept trying to get up, which with a back injury could do more damage. We will let you know when he is being transferred, but you should probably start making plans to go up to Fairview so you can be with him when he wakes up."

"Then you think he'll live," Mom asked.

The ER doctor hesitated, then replied cautiously, "We'll do everything in our power to make that happen, Mrs. Taylor. I can't promise."

A social worker took charge of us. Royal Valley Hospital was in Fairview, a larger city, about a hundred miles (I still thought in terms of miles, not kilometres) from Caribou.

"Do you have a car?"

"No," Mom replied. "My husband was in our pickup, which was our only transportation."

"You can take a bus. The city bus goes by on the street out here at ten after the hour, and will get you to the Greyhound terminal in five minutes."

"There's no way to fly?"

"No. Airlines in BC go east and west but not north and south. You would have to fly to Vancouver first."

Mom made a face. "Then, I assume there's a car rental company in town."

"Oh yes. Several of them."

So Mom rented a car, which we used for a couple of weeks while Dad was hospitalized in Fairview. Mom eventually bought a small car, using the insurance payment from his accident. We found a rental house in Caribou and went back there to get us kids into school for the rest of the year. Dad had several surgical procedures done, and when he was better, he would be transferred by air ambulance to a place in Vancouver that specialized in rehabilitation of people with spinal injuries.

It was several days before Dad was fully conscious of where he was, and who we were, when we visited. That was when I saw a new side of him that shocked and worried me. Once he understood that he would be a paraplegic, he exploded with anger of the 'why should this happen to me' type. He raged almost all the time during our visits. Mom resolved not to tell him to his face that if he had paid attention to the advice he had been given, it wouldn't have happened. She admonished us not to say anything about that either. However, after about the tenth time her visits started with Dad's snarl, "Why me?" I could see her resolve not to remind him waver and almost give way. It made our visits increasingly more uncomfortable, so that Penny and I hated to go.

During the long hours we spent at Dad's bedside, I had lots of time to think about what had happened there in the Beaver Valley, and what I knew about the murder. I passed a little series of scenes through my mind, putting them together into a plausible whole; the moonlit night when Con Monke passed by with his pack string; two nights later when Grace Herman sent Penny out into the garden in the moonlight to pick berries; Grace telling Sgt. Ross that she had seen Con come out with his pack string (or had she only said that she saw him, not knowing that the time she had seen him was important?); the man who had come down toward the grow op and hastily retreated when he saw the cops uncovering the grave; the hasty departure of the men from the grow op; the proximity of Con's campsite to the shed that must have contained the radio; the closeness of the shed to the grow op site; the fact that Dad must not have called the police when I found the antenna and the shed; and finally, the sound of a snowmobile turning not right toward the Monke ranch, but left to go up into the hills toward the shed where the radio must still have been.

The day after Grace's death, I had chatted with the Mounties when they came out in their chopper, and I had ridden all the way to Caribou with them, but I had said not one word about what I knew.

Why?

Because I didn't want to be the person who gave them the information that would have resulted in the arrest of the man who had saved my father's life.

Chapter Forty-Two

Penny and I had no trouble adjusting to regular school when we joined our respective classes after their spring break. It seemed that the English teacher who had guided my schooling had read my essays on 'the simple life' to her regular class at school, so my new classmates felt that they already knew me. Penny had the same experience.

Mom bought bikes for us, and for herself. Mine wasn't the racing bike I'd wanted, but a more practical type. But that was okay. I got into sports in a big way. We also got computers. We had to catch up on all the new stuff you could do with computers, but we picked it up easily. Mom balked at cell phones, however. She was especially dismayed at the possibility that we would go around with our heads down, constantly texting our friends. She shouldn't have worried. Penny and I both were so happy to be actually talking to, and doing things with, other kids that we had no trouble agreeing with Mom on that one.

Mom got a job as receptionist at a dental clinic with four dentists, including the one who had given me the lecture about smokeless tobacco. The regular receptionist was going on maternity leave, but even when she came back, Mom was kept on. In two years, she worked up to office manager. So we had an income even though Dad's had dried up. He made no effort to continue his work, though he had plenty of time to do it, and it was something he could still have done in spite of his disability.

When summer came, I got onto a baseball team. We, as a family, biked around the area, learning about the local recreation sites. On the whole, it was a happy time, if we could forget the problems our dad was facing—and how he was dealing, or not dealing, with them.

One day shortly after we moved into our house in Caribou, we ran into Sgt. Ross in the supermarket parking lot. He asked how we were getting along and about how Dad was. Mom, in turn, asked him how his investigation into the Beaver Creek murder was coming along.

"I heard you had picked up a suspect," she said.

"Yes. We found the radio the pot growers were using, and have traced it to Conner Monke. He denies having anything to do with the murder, but we know for sure that he is one of the associates of those men who lived at that grow op. We picked up a man living in Arrow who has a lumber truck and is the one taking the stuff across the border in loads of lumber, designated for a particular hardware store in Washington. That man has been picked up also, and the American police are still looking for those two men who lived in the cabin at the grow-op site.

"As for the murder, it had to be either Monke or one of those men who pulled the trigger, but we won't know until we talk to them."

I asked tentatively, "How did you find the radio?" I was by then pretty sure Dad had not passed my message along to the Mounties. Had they talked to him in the hospital and he remembered?

"We were waiting for someone to start using the radio again, so we left our equipment to record calls and get a second line of position, and the equipment recorded the call that was made to get help for Mrs. Herman and your dad. We got that second line of position we needed, and it indicated a spot at the top of the cliff above Arrow. We went up there to make a thorough search and found a building that had once held the radio, though the radio has since been taken out. The antenna is still there. They were in a grove of trees near the top of the cliff. There was a path from it to Monke's campsite, and on down to the grow op. When we picked up Monke, we found a citizens band radio stashed in a shed at his campsite. We can't prove it's the same radio, but it's pretty suggestive.

"So, everything fits. The only fly in the ointment is the discrepancy between your account, Derek, of Conner Monke coming out with his pack string late that night and Grace Herman's saying they came by her place that afternoon."

Should I say anything? I'd sworn not to tell the cops anything that would point to Con Monke. But I was just as boastful as anyone else my age. I abandoned my self-imposed oath and spoke up.

"Did she really say she saw them that afternoon, or did she just say she saw Con go by with his pack string?"

Ross paused before he answered. "I don't remember for sure. Why would it matter? Besides, she said she was working in her garden, and she wouldn't have been out in her garden at night."

"Oh yes she would. On Sunday night, only two days later, when there was still a full moon, Penny and I were over there at the Hermans' and Grace told Penny to go out in the garden and pick some blackberries. She said you could see well enough in the moonlight, and she sometimes worked in her garden when there was a full moon."

"That's right," Penny chipped in. "It was easy."

Ross wasn't fully convinced. "But she'd have seen that our man wasn't with him."

"Not necessarily," I countered. "She was probably so used to seeing Con go by with pack horses that she didn't pay much attention to it, but only remembered that he'd gone past."

"Maybe you're right. I'll have to ask Mr. Herman if he remembers anything about it."

Something Sgt. Ross had said earlier stuck in my mind. "You told me back when I talked to you out there on Beaver Creek, that there wasn't any trail down that hillside where I saw that guy. Now you're telling me there was a trail down from the place where you found the antenna."

"There was a clear trail from that place, but it petered out when it started down the last slope. We figured that those guys who used it made a point of taking different paths down that hill so they wouldn't leave a distinct trail that could be followed back up to the cliff. We just didn't search far enough. Once we found the place where they had the radio, we were able to follow the trail from there."

"Yeah, I know how some of those game trails peter out when you follow them. Thanks for telling me."

Penny had a question for Sgt. Ross. "Are you absolutely sure Con was the one who made that call for help?"

"We are. Harry, the man who heard the call and passed the message along, said he recognized the voice as the one that made the previous calls from that radio. He has listened to a lot of voices over the years, and is very good at recognizing them, so we recorded Monke's voice and had Harry listen to it. He was sure it was the same voice."

"Well, if he made that call, he's the one who saved our Dad's life, so if it's okay, my brother and I want to send him a card thanking him."

"That's right," I added. "Even if he committed a crime, it was still great of him to make that radio call. And I don't think Con did the murder. He's not like that."

"I wish I had your trust in humanity, Derek. And Penny, I don't see why you shouldn't send him a thank-you card."

As we parted from Sgt. Ross, I mulled over what he said about Con's part in the murder. I wanted to think that Con had not been the one to shoot the cop, but had only been an unwilling participant. He may not have realized, when he threw in with those grow-op guys, that violence might be involved. Grace Herman thought of him as a 'nice boy,' and hoped his budding business as an outfitter and guide would be successful. Steve Carlssen, on the other hand, had nothing good to say about any of the Monke men. I preferred to believe Grace. And there was no doubt Con Monke had tried to help both Grace and Dad when he made that radio call.

Chapter Forty-Three

It was the Victoria Day weekend before we could get back to our Beaver Valley home to pack up our belongings and move for good to the city. The water levels had receded, leaving mud and debris in our pasture. The wooden bridge over the creek had held up against the high water, but the road needed to be reworked and new gravel applied. There were many reminders of the flood.

Mom had been approached by a real estate agent willing to buy our place out there. She got a lawyer to deal with him, and he got her a better price than Mom could have gotten on her own. This would be the last trip to the valley where we had lived for nearly two years.

Mom hired two husky young men with a small cube van to come help us move. We didn't have a lot of furniture, and no kitchen appliances to move. We gave the wood-burning kitchen stove to Steve Carlssen in payment for all the care he had lavished on the livestock.

He groomed the horses before we came, brushing out the last of their thick winter hair, and leaving them glossy in their summer coats. He had even trimmed their hooves. We took the horses' shoes off at the beginning of the winter, since we would be riding very little, and in the spring the new hoof growth needed to be trimmed back and the horses shod. Mom had arranged to sell the horses and saddles back to Monke, against our vigorous requests to keep the horses and trailer them to Caribou. Mom had checked prices for boarding horses in Caribou and quickly vetoed our request. Monke would have to shoe them himself. We weren't going to call the farrier to come out here when we were just going to sell the horses.

On the day we went back to our home, Penny and I saddled up the horses and went for one last ride around the valley. The first place we went was the Hermans' house. It was closed up and looked deserted. Steve told us that Bill's daughter had come out, dragged Bill off with her and sold the ranch.

"Bill won't like living in a city," he said sadly.

He also told us that he knew a family in Arrow who would buy the cow and calf from us. The cow had her new calf beside her. It was the Jersey colour, a rich brown, but with a white face like the Herford bull. Penny on seeing the calf began to regret our move to the city, but Steve squelched that. "They grow up, you know. They aren't cute calves forever."

We stayed overnight, having left the beds to be dismantled and loaded on the truck last. The young men brought sleeping bags and unrolled them on the grass under the stars. Knowing that there would be no food in the house, Mom brought some with her for our supper and breakfast. She gave Steve the keys to the house and told him that when we were gone, to take all the food in the house for his own use.

Mowser was nowhere around. "I left food out for him, but I think the marmots and gophers probably ate most of it," Steve told us.

The next day, we rode Blaze and Peanuts over the bridge and up the road to the Monke ranch, carefully avoiding saying anything to Abe Monke about Con's arrest. As we unsaddled the horses in the barn, I felt something rub against my leg. I looked down and there was Mowser. Monke said, "Yeah, Big Red came back over here the day after you folks left."

I hadn't known that he'd been the Monkes' cat before he came over to our place. I offered to give Monke the remains of the bag of cat food. He shrugged. "We never bother to feed the barn cats. They get enough mice." No wonder Mowser was skinny when I saw him that day I first squirted milk into his mouth. But it wouldn't be good to take him with us. We lived on a main street in town. He would not have been happy confined to the house, and wouldn't know how to navigate the city streets.

Before we drove away from our old home, Penny and I had one last thing to do. We got a bucket and went to the spring. We scooped up the frog, carried him to the creek and turned him loose.

When we last drove out of the valley for that last time, Penny watched behind the car for a final glimpse of the place, but I had my eyes set straight ahead. Good riddance, as far as I was concerned.

Chapter Forty-Four

It was the beginning of my first year in high school when the blow-up with Dad occurred. It was my turn to go with Mom to visit Dad and I was bursting with news about high school, to say nothing of finally being able to take credit for solving a crime. To my dismay, it all blew up in my face.

Dad was waiting in the small room set aside for patients to meet privately with visitors. We went in with smiles on our faces, trying as usual to look and sound upbeat. Dad greeted us with his customary snarling complaints. I thought that news of my successes might cheer him up, so I launched on a description of my first few days in high school.

I met my new science teacher, realizing that if it hadn't been for Old Stoneface's arrest, that's who would have been my teacher. What a horrid thought! Anyway, the new teacher, on hearing that I wanted to be an engineer, arranged for me to spend a day with a local engineering firm on one of the teachers' professional development days, when there wouldn't be any classes. I told all this to Dad. His reaction was totally unexpected.

"You can forget about being an engineer, Derek. We won't be able to afford to send you to college. You'd better take a carpentry course while you're in school. Then you can go to work right out of school and make a decent living."

"I don't want to be a carpenter. I want to be an engineer."

"Well, forget about it. And Penny had better forget about being a nurse. I'll need a lot of expensive stuff. I need a motorized wheelchair and I'll have to get a van that's equipped with a lift. And we'll have to equip our house with hoists and runners along the ceiling. Those things cost the earth. They shouldn't, but the manufacturers know they have a captive group of people who will pay for stuff or be stuck forever without being able to go anywhere."

"We can afford those things," Mom said. She knew that Dad was making some progress in his rehabilitation, and might someday be able to walk again, but his progress was slow, and he would still need mobility aids for the foreseeable future.

"I don't see how. You don't know anything about business Liz. You don't know how much those things cost."

That stung Mom. She'd spent hours on our future budget to determine how much cash we would need to spend in the near future, and how much we could put away in investments. We had received a significant insurance payout as well as money from the sale of our land. She tried to go over her figures with Dad, but he just waved her account aside. "You don't know what you're talking about, Liz. It takes a man to understand that stuff."

Mom looked like a volcano about to erupt, but managed to get herself under control. She had learned by now that it didn't do any good to argue with Dad. She would just go home and do things her way. I stepped into the breach, which turned out not to be a good idea.

"You don't need to worry Dad. I have money."

"And just how do you think you can make enough money working for some fast food place to afford a college education? Besides, I'll have to use the money that got put aside for your education to get the stuff I need."

"You can't do that," Mom cried. "That is Derek's and Penny's money."

"You're forgetting, Liz, who made that money. That money is mine."

"You can't do that! Don't you care at all about your own children?"

Dad didn't answer. He knew that anything he said would be the wrong thing. I barged in again.

"But Dad, I already have the money."

"And where did you get all that money? Did you steal it or did you win a lottery?"

"That's not fair to make accusations like that," Mom told him.

"Hold on a minute," I almost shouted. "Let me explain."

"Well, it had better be good," Dad grumbled.

"Do you remember Mr. Stone?"

"Of course I remember Stone. What's he got to do with it?"

"Well, I was in his shop one time." I hoped Dad wouldn't ask how I got into the shop. I'd had to tell Mom, but I didn't dare tell Dad. "And I saw one of those letter bombs he was making."

I needn't have worried. Dad latched onto something else. "How would you know what a bomb looked like?"

"Before we moved up here, when we were going to public school," I explained, "a policeman came to talk to us about things that we might find that we shouldn't touch. Along with other stuff, he showed us some types of explosives and detonators. I saw something that was exactly like one of those types of explosives, and also one of the detonators, there in Stone's shop."

"So that makes you an expert?" He made it sound as if he thought I was an idiot.

Ignoring that barb, I went on, "Remember when he would go to town for several days, and when he came back he'd bring us a *Globe and Mail*, and you were always complaining about the news items that always seemed to be in it? One of those articles was about someone receiving a letter bomb. I think he had just mailed one of his bombs, and bringing us those newspaper accounts was his way of bragging about it.

"Anyway, when I was there in his shop I saw a list of names and addresses. The first three on that list were names of people that those articles reported as having gotten those bombs. There were two more names, and one of them was on the label of a package he was putting the bomb into. I memorized those two names and addresses, and the next time you went to town, I went with you and went to the pay phone at the entrance to the general store. They had a notice tacked up there about the TIP line, so I called the number and told the guy who answered about the bomb and gave him the names and addresses of the people on that list who hadn't gotten bombs yet. He told me that there was a twenty-five thousand dollar reward and that it had just been upped by another fifteen grand. If my information got used to convict Stone of the crime, I'd get forty thousand bucks."

Dad's face had been turning purple while I talked. Now he exploded.

"I can't believe a son of mine would be so greedy that he'd sell a man for a bunch of money. Stone is a good man. I'm pissed off that you'd do something like that. You're a regular Judas."

"But Dad, he was killing people."

"You don't know that he was. He's a good man."

"Well, he confessed…"

"If he did he was probably coerced."

"Dad, he got up in court and spouted off for over an hour about how those people deserved to die and he was glad he'd done it."

"I don't care. You're going to give that money back. No one in my family is going to benefit from blood money." Dad was shouting now, and a nurse stuck her head in the door. Mom apologized for the shouting then waved her away. The nurse withdrew, leaving us alone to have our family feud.

Mom took over. "Phil, he is *not* going to give the money back. He was acting as a responsible citizen. That man was dangerous."

"Well I'm going to call them and tell them we'll return the money."

"No, you won't. In the first place, you can't."

"Why can't I?"

Mom continued with her explanation. "The money has already been invested in a trust fund for Derek. They only needed one parent's signature as co-investor and that's me. Derek can't use it without my permission until he becomes an adult. That's just when he'll need it to go to university. And Derek has agreed that what you and I had put away for the kids' education should all go to Penney."

"I can't believe my whole family is turning against me. You're all just a bunch of greedy money-grabbers. I won't have it."

"Well Phil, you'll just have to put up with it. I'm leaving. And I'm not coming back!" She marched out the door. I followed behind her, but when I came to the door, I turned back.

"I'm sorry, Dad."

I went out, gently pulling the door shut behind me. That was the last time I ever visited my Dad.

Chapter Forty-Five

Those two guys who lived in the cabin at the grow op were eventually caught by the police in Washington and extradited to Canada. The Mounties charged Con Monke with lesser crimes, and he was out on bail until they had a chance to interview those two guys. Con admitted to being in on the pot operation, and also to catching the undercover cop snooping around the shed that held the radio, overpowering him, tying him up and marching him down to the grow op. He claimed that he did not know the man was a cop, and said he thought the 'miners' would only give him a lecture, and maybe rough him up a little for snooping around their property. Con was also the man I'd seen walking down the hillside and had turned around and hurried away. He said he'd been going to the cabin to make certain the 'miners' hadn't left anything that could point to him.

He vehemently denied killing the cop, accusing one of those two men who lived in the cabin of pulling the trigger. When caught, they tried to blame it on Con. But Con claimed to have been appalled by the murder, and I thought he was probably telling the truth. I hoped the police would think so, too, and I guess they believed him enough that they accepted his story over that of the fake miners.

Con was a rancher and licenced outfitter and guide with a good reputation, whose only previous scrape with the law was selling marijuana cigarettes to a few friends. But what really stood Con in good stead with the police was that the cops knew that it was Con who made that radio call that brought help for Grace and Dad. He had risked his own freedom to help two neighbours in distress, and that weighed in his favour.

Those other guys, on the other hand, had numerous run-ins with the law, and the one Con fingered had been convicted previously of violent crimes. He was also the one Mom identified as the man who threatened her and Grandpa when they went fishing out there at the grow op. It made her shudder when she saw him on TV. The police charged him with first-degree murder, and charged Con and the other man with less serious offences. They are all in prison now, but Con has applied for day parole and will probably get it.

Several years after we left the Beaver Valley, I ran into Steve Carlssen on the street in Caribou. His pretty wife was with him, and the little girl who had been his first baby was prancing along ahead of them. Steve was carrying a baby, and his wife, who was pregnant again, was leading a toddler by the hand. "This next one is a girl," she told me. "That will give us two boys and two girls so we're going to stop."

Steve brought me up-to-date on events in the valley. "Remember, I told you that Bill's daughter dragged him off to live with her? Anyhow, a couple of months later he had a heart attack and died. He might have had the heart attack anyway, even if he'd stayed on his ranch, but he'd have been a lot happier. The daughter sold out to some guy named Bigelow, but I've never seen him out there."

Steve asked me if I remembered Woody Woodrow and I assured him I did. "He used to walk along side those logs he was skidding, but I guess his reflexes weren't so good any more, and one time he missed his step and a log rolled on his leg. It was good luck that it happened when someone was with him, because it was a pretty bad break, and if he'd been alone, he'd have laid there until someone found the horses and went looking for him. Anyway, after his leg healed, he had a stroke. He's now in a nursing home and he loves it. He has all the old women there fawning over him, and the staff all love him. By the way, he remembers you as 'that family what lived in a tent.'"

I had a good chuckle at the thought of that old guy who spoke in monosyllables making up to the old ladies.

"You know that Con's in jail, don't you?" I nodded. "Well, the Monkes sold their livestock and the ranch, and moved out, but nobody knows where they went. I expect that the younger boy, Chad, may be in jail by now. He was a bad one. There's nobody living out there in the valley any more."

While we were talking, the little girl came up to me and asked, "Are you an uncle?"

Steve noticed the perplexed look on my face and laughed. "We told Hailey that she could call family friends Auntie or Uncle. She hasn't quite figured out which is which. Do you remember Darlene?"

"I never met her, but I know who you're talking about."

"Well she came out with her kids to see her folks before they left, and Hailey called her 'Uncle Darlene,' and Darlene laughed her head off. By the way she's still married and has several kids. Her man has a good job, so they're doing okay."

Hailey was still waiting for my answer. I squatted down to get nearer her level. "Hello Hailey. Yes, I'm Uncle Derek." The girl clapped her hands and said happily, "I got it right."

Chapter Forty-Six

I'm now in the last year of my engineering course and will get my degree in the spring. Penny is in the Bachelor of Nursing course and is the top student in her class. She sees Dad from time to time, and says he's getting better both physically and mentally, and that he's re-started his editing business.

The summer before my final year, the advisor in charge of finding summer placements for engineering students gave me a choice between two jobs. One was to work with a company building a replacement bridge over a major river where the traffic flow had become too great for the existing bridge to handle. The other was to help build a high-class resort in a mountain valley in southern British Columbia. The advisor gave me a copy of the advertising brochure for this proposed resort.

"Take a look at this one, Derek. I'll be back in a few minutes."

The glossy brochure offered a 'wilderness retreat where you can enjoy the beauty of nature in five-star comfort.' The lodge would have an Olympic size swimming pool, spas, a fitness centre, and a ballroom. Outdoors, there would be an eighteen-hole golf course designed by a leading golf course designer, an equestrian centre with facilities to host events such as show jumping and dressage, and an outdoor stage for musical events. There would also be a fishing pool where you would be guaranteed to catch fish. I suspected that the fish hooks would be baited with the food that was fed to the captive trout, and that the fishing would be done before the fish were fed so that they would be hungry. It would probably be like those places where tame deer in an enclosed pasture were 'hunted' by men who paid big money to do so. I'm disgusted with things like that.

The road into the resort would be paved and electricity and phone services supplied, along with wi-fi and high-speed Internet. "Some wilderness," I snorted. "They probably wouldn't even notice the scenery, they'd have their noses too deeply buried in their laptops, or be sound asleep in their air-conditioned bedrooms, with all the draperies drawn."

I turned back to the cover where I'd briefly noted the name of the outfit that was building this resort. There it was; Beaver Valley Lodge. To be built by Bigelow Properties, Ltd. The guy who had bought our place and the Hermans' and presumably Stone's and the Monkes'.

The lodge would be built at the site of the Monke ranch buildings. The top end of the valley, where the Hermans lived would become the equestrian area. A parking lot and gazebo would be built at a viewpoint on the property that now held Old Stoneface's cabin. Our horse pasture would be the sixteenth hole of the championship golf course. The creek would be dredged, straightened and lined with rock, with decorative little bridges crossing it at intervals. At the place where I'd fallen off the log, there would be an artificial waterfall.

I didn't want to think about what would happen to the beavers and their lodge. Bigelow Properties, Ltd. should at least have preserved the namesake of their fancy resort, I thought. And the gophers, those pesky little critters who dug holes that horses stepped in, and sat up on their haunches beside their dens laughing at us, would probably be brutally evicted. A fence, high enough to prevent deer jumping over it would surround the entire property.

In essence they were going to destroy the very things that created the wilderness they were advertising, and to top it off they were going to eliminate all the wild animals from their wilderness!

These people were interlopers. They didn't belong. This valley belonged to the does with their spindly fawns and the predators who hunted them; to the beavers industriously working on their dam; to the trout lazing in the deep pools of the creek; to the hawks circling overhead looking for unwary prey; even to the pesky gophers. Even the range cattle didn't seem out of place. We—our family and the other people who had lived out there—had been interlopers ourselves, but we'd had minimal impact on the wilderness while we lived there. Once this resort was built, the only vestige of wilderness left would be the view. But when I envisioned that view in my mind's eye, I saw only storm clouds rolling down the northwestern mountain slopes.

I hoped that maybe a big orange and white cat would come to the door of the fancy kitchen asking for a chicken wing, and on holidays, if the chef was a nice guy, maybe be given a spoonful of caviar.

The adviser walked back into the room and saw me looking at the brochure. "Pretty neat, eh? You'll be taking the job at that development, won't you?"

I flipped the brochure into the wastebasket. "No," I said, "I think I'll take the bridge job."

The End

About the Author

Anne Barton is a retired veterinarian and flight instructor. In her retirement, she has taken up writing mystery novels. She has also written one autobiographical book and numerous articles and short stories. Her short story won the Bloody Words Crime Writers' Conference contest in 2001 and is published in Bloody Words, The Anthology.

Born in Drumheller, Alberta, she grew up in Northern Idaho, returned to Canada, and now lives in the beautiful Okanagan Valley in British Columbia, where she is deeply involved with Habitat for Humanity and her Anglican Church work – that is, when she isn't riding horses or curling.

www.annebartonmysteries.ca
www.mysterycarolyndale.ca
Author photo by Maia MacDonald

THE SIMPLE LIFE IS MURDER

CPSIA information can be obtained
at www.ICGtesting.com
Printed in the USA
LVHW04s2253170518
577647LV00001B/2/P